A TAFFY NIGHTMARE

I was in bed, but I was wide awake, tossing and turning and trying to get to sleep. Finally I closed my eyes and when I did, there she was. Taffy Sinclair. And she was laughing so hard that you could see her one crooked bicuspid. It was at Mama Mia's Pizzeria after the football game on Saturday afternoon, and Taffy was standing beside the table where Randy and I were sitting. She was pointing at me while she laughed, and suddenly she turned around and shouted to all the other kids, "Jana Morgan can't even talk to Randy because her tongue is numb!"

I thought I'd die. What good would it do to be the first girl in the sixth grade to have a date with Randy Kirwan, the most wonderful boy in the world, if Taffy Sinclair was going to spoil it?

I'd get that Taffy Sinclair. I'd get her if it was the last thing I ever did.

D0109268

Bantam Skylark Books by Betsy Haynes
Ask your bookseller for the books you have missed

THE AGAINST TAFFY SINCLAIR CLUB
TAFFY SINCLAIR STRIKES AGAIN
TAFFY SINCLAIR, QUEEN OF THE SOAPS
TAFFY SINCLAIR AND THE ROMANCE MACHINE
   DISASTER
THE GREAT MOM SWAP

TAFFY SINCLAIR AND THE ROMANCE MACHINE DISASTER

Betsy Haynes

A BANTAM SKYLARK BOOK®

TORONTO · NEW YORK · LONDON · SYDNEY · AUCKLAND

RL 5, 009–012

TAFFY SINCLAIR AND THE ROMANCE MACHINE DISASTER

A Bantam Skylark Book / April 1987
2nd printing . . . June 1988

Skylark Books is a registered trademark of Bantam Books,
a division of Bantam Doubleday Dell Publishing Group, Inc.
Registered in U.S. Patent and Trademark Office and elsewhere.

All rights reserved.
Copyright © 1987 by Betsy Haynes.
Cover art copyright © 1987 by Bantam Books.
No part of this book may be reproduced or transmitted
in any form or by any means, electronic or mechanical,
including photocopying, recording, or by any information
storage and retrieval system, without permission in
writing from the publisher.
For information address: Bantam Books.

ISBN 0-553-15644-6

Published simultaneously in the United States and Canada

Bantam Books are published by Bantam Books, a division of Bantam Doubleday
Dell Publishing Group, Inc. Its trademark, consisting of the words "Bantam
Books" and the portrayal of a rooster, is Registered in U.S. Patent and
Trademark Office and in other countries. Marca Registrada. Bantam Books,
666 Fifth Avenue, New York, New York 10103.

PRINTED IN THE UNITED STATES OF AMERICA

S   11 10 9 8 7 6 5 4

For Judy Johnasen Correll

1 ✻

"**W**hen Taffy Sinclair hears the news, she'll be so jealous she'll absolutely die."

My four best friends all looked at me as if I'd totally lost my mind.

"What news?" demanded Beth Barry. "Jana, what on earth are you talking about?"

I just smiled mysteriously. I was dying to blurt it out, but I didn't, even though it was the most exciting thing that had happened in my entire life.

"I hate to say this," said Katie Shannon, "but I can't think of a single reason for Taffy Sinclair to be jealous of you."

I knew what Katie was thinking. Taffy Sinclair has long blond hair and big blue eyes and is the most gorgeous girl in the sixth grade at Mark Twain Elementary. Of course she is also the snottiest and most stuck-up person in the entire world. Besides that, she is my biggest enemy, and we've had clubs against each other and have been rivals for more things than I like to remember. But now I, Jana Morgan, finally had something she didn't have. Something that I knew she wanted. That was why I had called my four best friends and announced a special meeting of our self-improvement club, the Fabulous Five, so that I could break the news to everyone at once.

"Come on, Jana. Don't keep us in suspense." Christie Winchell clasped her hands and held them up as if she were begging. "Tell us before we all explode."

I was the one who was ready to explode, and so I took a deep breath and said, "Randy Kirwan called me a few minutes ago and asked me to watch his football game Saturday afternoon and then go out with him for pizza afterward."

All four of my best friends' mouths dropped open at once, and it got totally quiet in my bedroom. Randy Kirwan is the handsomest and most popular boy in school, and I have had a secret crush on him for ages. My friends knew about my crush on Randy, but they didn't know that for a while I kept a picture of him hidden under a poster of Miss Piggy on the wall beside my bed with a night light under it. That way I could take down the Miss Piggy poster when I went to bed at night, turn on the night light, and look at his handsome face while I fell asleep.

Suddenly Beth jumped up and put her face so close to mine that our noses were practically touching. "When did he ask you? What did he say? Tell us all about it!" she shrieked. Then she fell across my bed so hard that she bounced three times. "I can't believe it!" she said. "Randy Kirwan asked you for a date. You're the first girl in the sixth grade to have a date with a boy. You're even ahead of Taffy Sinclair!"

I nodded triumphantly. "As soon as we hung up, I called this meeting to tell you all about it."

"You're right about Taffy. She'll absolutely turn green when she sees you together Saturday," said Christie. "She's such a flirt, always hanging around him and making him talk to her."

A picture of Taffy flirting with Randy flashed across my mind, making my face red and my ears hot. Christie was right. She does it all the time, flipping her long blond hair over her shoulder and rolling her big blue eyes. It's obvious to everybody that she has a huge crush on him, too. Suddenly I knew that I couldn't wait until Saturday.

"Everybody help me think," I said. "We've got to come up with a way to let Taffy know about Randy and me before Saturday. We've got to make her suffer and be jealous and wish that she was going out with Randy instead of me."

"One of us could call her on the phone right now," suggested Melanie.

Christie was nodding and grinning like crazy. "And whoever did it could disguise her voice so Taffy wouldn't know who it was."

I didn't say anything. I really wanted to see her face when she found out. Still, it wasn't such a bad idea.

"I'll call her," said Beth. "I can disguise my voice so that she'll never know it's me. Come on, Jana. Let me call her."

When I still didn't say anything, Beth added, "Then when we all go home we can call a bunch of other girls and tell them, and by the time you get to school in the morning, you'll be a celebrity."

"Okay," I said. "You convinced me."

I handed Beth the phone and felt tingles race up and down my spine as we all watched her dial. She held the receiver away from her ear so that we could hear it ringing, and I clamped a hand over my mouth and swallowed a giggle as a tiny voice said, "Hello."

Beth sucked in her cheeks, raised her eyebrows and looked down at the mouthpiece wearing a very serious expression. Then she said in her best fake English accent, "Hello, dahling. May I puh-lease speak to Taffy Sinclai-ah."

It was a super accent, and Melanie and I nodded excitedly to each other.

"Taffy, *dahling*, is that you?" Then she winked and we almost broke up laughing.

"I have some absolutely *fabulous* news, dahling. Jana Morgan has a *date* with Randy Kirwan after the football game Saturday afternoon."

Beth held the receiver toward us again, and we could hear Taffy Sinclair as plain as anything. "That's a big fat lie. Who is this, anyway?"

By now Beth was starting to giggle. "A lie! That's what you think," she sputtered, completely losing her accent.

"Hang up," Katie insisted, "before she figures out that it's us."

Beth dropped the receiver back into the cradle and we spent the next five minutes talking about how jealous Taffy must be.

When everyone had stopped talking about Taffy, Melanie said, "Taffy's not the only one who's jealous. I think it's so romantic that Randy asked you out. It's just like on television."

"Oh, no. This is not a soap opera," I said quickly. I was thinking about all those people on the soap operas my friends and I started watching when Taffy Sinclair got that teensy little part in *Interns and Lovers* and about all the terrible things that happened to them. "This is the real thing. Randy even said so."

Christie's eyes got wide with excitement. "You've got to be kidding," she groaned ecstatically.. "He said he loves you?"

"Well, not exactly," I admitted. "Not those very words, anyway. What he said was that he really admires me. That means he thinks I'm a kind and sensitive person like he is and that we have a lot in common."

"That's certainly a relief," said Melanie. "At least if you have a lot in common you'll have things to talk about. You don't know how lucky you are. I always freeze up when I'm around cute boys. I can't think of a thing to say. It's awful," she said. "Not only does my mind go blank so that I just stare into space like a dummy, but MY TONGUE GOES NUMB!"

I gave Melanie a sympathetic look. She was on a diet and getting thin and a lot prettier now, but for the longest time she stuffed herself with anything edible, especially brownies, and was terribly overweight. It was no wonder that she had trouble talking to cute boys.

A few minutes later my friends went home, promising to call everyone they could think of to tell them about my date with Randy. I was glad when they left because I was suddenly getting nervous. I had never worried about talking to Randy Kirwan, but then I had never had a date with him before either. Now that Melanie had brought up the subject, I couldn't think of a single thing to talk about. Good grief, I thought. This was already Thursday afternoon. Saturday and the football game were only two days away. Surely I could think of something to talk to Randy about by then. I'd rack my brain until I thought of something really clever. I'd make the most brilliant conversation Randy had ever heard. But secretly, I could already feel my tongue going numb.

Later, at the dinner table, I told Mom my big news. "Guess what?" I chirped. "Randy Kirwan wants me to watch him play football Saturday and then go for pizza. Is it okay if I go?"

Mom gave me a funny look for a minute. It was probably her "how can my little girl be grown up enough to be going on a date" look, but it was gone almost as fast as it had come and she was smiling again. "I think that's wonderful, Jana. Of course you can go, and I'm sure you'll have a great time. Randy is a very nice boy."

You can say that again, I thought. Nice and cute and a terrific football player, but what on earth would we talk about? We couldn't talk about how nice he was or how cute, and I didn't know anything about football. At least not enough to make a conversation. I thought maybe Mom would have some suggestions, but when I asked her, she gave me a quick hug and said, "Don't worry about it, honey. Just be yourself, and you'll think of lots of things to talk about."

That was easy for her to say. Still, as I watched her secretly out of the corner of my eye, I couldn't help wondering what she and Pink talked about. Pink is short for Wallace Pinkerton, and he's her boyfriend. Actually, he's more than just a boyfriend. He bought her a diamond ring and asked her to marry him, but Mom says she needs more time to make up her mind. Mom and my father have been divorced for a long time, but she doesn't want to rush into anything. Anyway, I kept thinking about Mom and Pink. I couldn't imagine Mom's tongue *ever* going numb. Whenever Pink is over at our apartment, she always talks up a storm. But for the life of me, I couldn't remember what they talked about.

After we finished washing the dishes I pretended to do my homework, but my mind was still on my tongue. I rolled it around in my mouth and thought about it. I kept remembering how it felt last summer when Dr. Anderson gave me a shot of Novocain before he filled my tooth. It was awful. I could barely talk, and I definitely couldn't eat. Eat! I thought. How could I possibly eat pizza with Randy if my tongue was numb? What if I tried to take a bite of pizza and bit my tongue instead? I'd be so embarrassed that I'd die.

That night I had a dream about Taffy Sinclair. It wasn't the kind of dream you have when you're asleep. I was in bed, but I was wide awake, tossing and turning and trying to get comfortable. My sheets and blankets were a mess and my pillow felt like a rock. I couldn't go to sleep, but finally I closed my eyes and when I did, there she was. As real as anything. And she was laughing so hard that you could see her one crooked bicuspid. It was at Mama Mia's Pizzeria after the football game on Saturday afternoon, and Taffy was standing beside the table where Randy and I were sitting. She was pointing at me while she laughed, and suddenly she turned around and shouted to all the other kids in Mama Mia's, "Jana Morgan can't even talk to Randy because her tongue is numb!"

I thought I'd die. What good would it do to be the first girl in the sixth grade to have a date with Randy Kirwan, the most wonderful boy in the world, if Taffy Sinclair was going to spoil it? In my dream I could hear everybody laughing. I couldn't look at Randy. I didn't want to know if he was laughing, too. I'd get that Taffy Sinclair. I'd get her if it was the last thing I ever did.

2 ✳

*B*eth had been right. I was a celebrity. When I got to school the next morning girls came running up to ask me about my big date.

"Is it true? Is it true?" shrieked Alexis Duvall. "Do you really have a date with Randy Kirwan?"

By the time I could even begin to answer Alexis, a crowd had already gathered around me. I tried to act casual, as if this sort of thing happened to me every day of the week.

"It's true," I said. "Randy called me yesterday afternoon and asked me to watch his football game tomorrow and then go out for pizza with him afterward."

"Oh, Jana! You're so lucky," cried Kim Baxter. She rolled her eyes backwards and wobbled her knees as if she were going to faint, but I knew she was only faking.

"Randy Kirwan is so-o-o-o cute," said Sara Sawyer. "I'd give anything to have a date with him."

There were murmurs of "Yeah," and "So would I." I fought hard to keep a big fat smile from spreading across my face. I had to admit that it was fun being a celebrity. There was only one thing wrong. I couldn't find Taffy Sinclair anywhere. I was dying to see her face.

"Listen. I have to go now," I said. "I'll talk to you later."

I started moving away in the direction of my friends, but Kim caught my hand, stopping me. "You've got to promise that you'll tell us everything that happens on your date. Promise?" she begged. She had such a grip on my hand that I knew I'd better promise or I'd never get away from her.

"Sure. I promise to tell you all about it."

I darted away from them before someone else had a great idea and grabbed me again. I wanted to talk to my friends and ask them if they'd seen Taffy Sinclair. I was walking across the school ground toward them when disaster struck.

"Hi, Jana!"

Oh, no, I thought. This can't be happening to me, today of all days. It was nerd of the world, Curtis Trowbridge. I ignored the alligator-size grin on Curtis's face and tried not to remember how he had been following me around for practically a whole year acting as if he were my boyfriend. Not only that, but Curtis was so brainy that he lived on another planet. What if Randy saw me talking to him? Would he think I really *liked* Curtis?

Curtis came trotting up beside me with his glasses bouncing on his nose. "Going to your locker? I'll walk with you."

Great, I thought. Now what would I do? For an instant I thought about sending him off on a wild goose chase, tracking down an imaginary idea for a story for the *Mark Twain Sentinel*. Curtis takes being sixth-grade editor for the school newspaper pretty seriously. He would do anything to get a story. But then I changed my mind. I couldn't do a thing like that to Curtis. Underneath that brainy exterior was a pretty nice person, and I really didn't want to hurt his feelings. Besides, I wanted Randy to see me as the kind and sensitive person that I really am.

"I'll walk as far as the front door with you," I offered. "My friends are waiting for me there."

I fell in step with him just as he whipped out a notebook and pencil. "What was all the excitement about?" he asked. "You really drew a crowd when you got to school. Is it anything that would make a good story for the paper?"

"Gosh, no. It was nothing," I blurted. Then I looked away so that Curtis couldn't see the blush spreading over my face. Knowing how Curtis felt about me, how could I tell him that all the excitement was because I was going out with Randy Kirwan?

Fortunately we had gotten to where my friends were standing. "See you later, Curtis," I said.

"Bye, Jana," Curtis said. "See you in class."

"Have you seen Taffy Sinclair?" asked Melanie. "We can't find her anywhere, and we're dying to see the look on her face this morning."

I shook my head and started scanning the school ground. I wanted to see her more than anyone, but she was nowhere in sight.

"I'll bet she's waiting until the first bell rings to show up," said Katie. "You know how she likes to make a grand entrance."

As if on cue, the first bell rang, and we scrambled to our room and took our seats. I didn't think Taffy Sinclair would ever get there. In fact, I was beginning to wonder if she was going to be absent. All the kids were in their seats, including Randy. He had come into the room with Mark Peters and Scott Daly, and they had been horsing around as usual, which is probably why he didn't look at me or say hi or anything. Anyway, Taffy finally got there, strutting to her seat as if she expected applause to break out any minute. My heart was pounding as she sat down at her desk. I held my breath as I waited to see what she would do.

You could tell she knew that she had an audience because she turned around very slowly in her seat and looked back over her shoulder and smiled. I knew who she was looking at, but still, when she said his name out loud I thought I would explode. "Hi, Randy," she said in her icky sweet voice.

I think I heard him say hi back to her, but my heart was pounding so loudly in my ears by then that I couldn't be sure. Then Taffy turned around the other way and looked over her shoulder at me. I thought I'd die. She was giving me the worst poison-dart look I had ever seen. It wasn't just her standard "drop dead" poison-dart look. It was an "I'll get even with you" look, if I ever saw one.

I scrunched down in my seat and hid behind my notebook, wondering how she planned to get even with me. I had never seen her looking so mad. Maybe letting Beth call her on the phone and disguise her voice to tell her about my date hadn't been such a good idea after all.

I peeked over my notebook at Randy to see if he was looking at me, too, but he wasn't. Not at first, anyway. But then he turned a little bit in his seat until he was looking in my direction. I thought that he might be looking out the window, which was also in my direction, and I tried to look away. I didn't want him to catch me staring at him and think I was a nerd. But suddenly he *was* looking at me—with both big blue eyes—and he was smiling that 1,000-watt smile that always makes my heart turn flip-flops. I tried to smile back, but my mouth had turned to Silly Putty, and I wasn't sure if the corners were pointing up or down. It didn't matter. What did matter was that he was smiling at me and not at Taffy Sinclair. I was so happy I thought I'd die.

❄ ❄ ❄

The crowd was already gathering when my friends and I got to the football field behind the junior high school the next afternoon. There were a lot of kids from Mark Twain Elementary in the bleachers on our side of the field, especially girls who came to watch all the cute boys play football. And there was Curtis Trowbridge pacing up and down the sidelines carrying a notebook and pencil and wearing a hand-lettered sign saying PRESS stuck to the front of his ski hat. Of course there was Taffy Sinclair prancing around by the concession stand, flirting with some boys from the other school and acting conceited the way she always does. But mostly there were parents. I had seen Randy's parents a couple of times, so I glanced across the crowd, trying to look as casual as possible, to see if I could spot them.

"Look, Jana! There are Randy's parents!" Melanie shouted. She was standing so close to me that she nearly blew my left ear right off.

I gave her a poison-dart look. "Shut up, Melanie," I growled. "They'll hear you and think it was me."

Fortunately, Mr. and Mrs. Kirwan had stopped to talk to some other parents and didn't hear Melanie. I tried not to stare at them as we followed Katie up the center stairs to the seats where most of the sixth-grade girls sat.

I looked up just as our team ran out onto the field wearing all-white uniforms. His number was twenty-two, and with his dark hair and eyes, Randy looked so handsome I thought I'd die. When they lined up in the middle of the field to warm up Randy looked over at the crowd in the bleachers and grinned when he saw me looking back. I smiled at him, too, and it felt as if my smile was stretching so big that it wrapped around behind my ears.

All through his warm-up Randy kept doing little eyeball maneuvers in my direction. I was just about to burst with happiness, and I sat there wondering if I could possibly live through the entire game. After a while I checked my tongue. It was still okay. So far, so good.

I watched more of that football game than all of the other ones I'd seen in my life put together. At first it scared me when Randy got tackled. What if he was hurt? What if he couldn't get up? What if I lost my chance to be the first girl in sixth grade to have a date? But after a while I started to relax, and just before the half Randy caught a pass and ran all the way to the end zone for a touchdown. The crowd went crazy, and I looked at Randy's father out of the corner of my eye. He had jumped up and was towering over everybody, waving his arms and yelling his head off.

Randy made two more touchdowns in the second half. I saw those, too, but also I kept watching the clock on the scoreboard and thinking about how nervous I was. I had never been alone with Randy before. Of course we wouldn't be totally alone. There would be tons of kids in Mama Mia's. But we would be alone when we walked from the football field to Mama Mia's. And we would sit at a table by ourselves. And we would walk home alone afterwards. And all that time, I would have to talk to him. What on earth was I going to say?

I tried to shut out the crowd noises as I thought about it. I closed my eyes and remembered all the daydreams I had had about Randy and me. We had been alone together in all of those. And we had plenty to say to each other in them, too. But what? I racked my brain, trying to ignore kids going wild and shouting all around me, but I couldn't remember a single thing we had talked about.

The game was over in what seemed like only a few minutes, and kids were jumping up and pouring out of the stands.

"We won!" shouted Katie. Then she gave me a big smile and asked, "How does it feel to have a date with the star of the game?"

"Great," I said, hoping no one would notice how nervous I was. "I'll see you guys later. Okay?"

"At Mama Mia's," chirped Christie. "We'll be watching for you and Randy to get there."

Then my four best friends left me standing all alone.

3 ✳

I was so nervous that my teeth were starting to chatter. I waited in the stands the way Randy had told me to do. He told me that he would be out of the gym just as soon as he took a shower and changed his clothes and then we would walk to Mama Mia's Pizzeria, which was only three blocks away.

It was a cold fall day, and I zipped up my jacket and watched the wind blow leaves around in circles along with empty popcorn boxes and mimeographed programs, and I worried all over again about what we would talk about. What if he wanted to talk about football and those three touchdowns? Sure, I had seen them, but my knowledge about football ended there. I could never fake a thing like that. Or maybe neither one of us would come up with anything to talk about and we would just sit and stare at each other all afternoon.

"Hi, Jana. Thanks for waiting."

"Oh," I said. "Hi, Randy." I was so deep in thought that I hadn't seen or heard Randy coming, but there he was, looking at me and smiling, water droplets sparkling in his dark hair. I felt better already. I could spend the rest of the day just looking at his kind and sensitive smile.

That smile gave me confidence I didn't know I had, so I got brave and said, "That was a great game, and those three touchdowns you made were really super."

Randy beamed. "Did you really think so?"

"Sure." I wanted to tell him how scared I had been when he was tackled, but I was afraid he might think I was being silly.

"Playing football really makes me hungry. I can't wait to get that bi-i-ig, juicy pizza. What kind of pizza do you like, anyway?"

"Deep-dish pepperoni, green pepper, and mushroom," I said.

"You're kidding." He looked at me as if he were in total shock. "That's my absolute favorite. I order it every time I go to Mama Mia's."

"Really?" I said, echoing his surprise. "So do I, but most kids I know won't go near green peppers and mushrooms."

"That's their tough luck. They don't know what they're missing."

Randy gave me a big grin, and I grinned back. I had been right. We did have things in common.

When we got to Mama Mia's it was so packed with kids that we could barely get in the front door, but once we got inside something really weird happened. All over the place kids stopped talking and stared at us. Especially the girls. I knew they were all imagining what it would be like to be walking into Mama Mia's with a date and how it would feel if that date were Randy Kirwan.

"Oh, hi, Randy. Why don't you sit here? We can squeeze in one more person."

Explosions went off in my heart. I'd know that voice anywhere. It was Taffy Sinclair, and she and Mona Vaughn were sitting at a big table with Mark Peters and Scott Daly, Randy's two best friends. Taffy was smiling at Randy and batting her eyelashes. It was her fake smile, the icky sweet one she always used on cute boys, but this time she was overdoing it. Beside her, poor ugly Mona Vaughn was trying to imitate Taffy's icky sweet smile. She was even trying to bat her eyelashes like Taffy. Usually I felt sorry for Mona since she worshiped the very ground Taffy walked on and followed her around as if she were Taffy's slave. But this time I was furious, even at Mona.

"Look, Randy. Someone's leaving over there," I said triumphantly. I was talking to him and pointing to a table where three high school boys were getting up, but

I was looking at Taffy Sinclair. She was looking back, and if looks could kill, we would both have been goners.

"Great," said Randy. "Thanks, Taffy. We'll see you later."

Over my dead body, I thought. Then I stuck my nose in the air and followed Randy to *our* table. Everyone had stopped staring at us and started talking again but not before they saw me get the best of Taffy Sinclair.

When the waitress stopped at our table, Randy ordered us a large deep-dish pepperoni, green pepper, and mushroom pizza and two large Cokes.

When the food came, I took a bite and strung the cheese out in front of me the way I always did, winding it back around my tongue. Across the table, Randy was doing the very same thing. I thought about Taffy Sinclair, and I was so happy I thought I'd die.

"What is your favorite animal?" He asked the question so abruptly that the Coke I was drinking almost snorted out my nose.

"I love dogs," I said. "But our landlord won't let us have one in the apartment."

"Dogs are my favorites, too. I have a dog named Heidi. She loves to play, and I'll bet you'd really like her."

My heart skipped a beat. I had seen Heidi once when I rode past his house on my bicycle. She was a keeshond, and she was definitely one of the most beautiful dogs I had ever seen. I couldn't believe it. Randy was practically asking me over to play with her.

The more we talked, the more we found we had in common, and we talked faster and faster, almost interrupting each other sometimes.

"I absolutely hate onions," said Randy.

"Me, too. And brussels sprouts. Do you like brussels sprouts?"

"Are you kidding? They're gross!" Randy made a face that was so funny I doubled over laughing.

We found out that we both love going to amusement parks and riding the roller coaster and going to the beach and watching fireworks on the Fourth of July. I couldn't remember when I'd had so much fun. I was glowing all over. And best of all, my tongue hadn't gone numb once.

Just then something caught my eye. It was Beth and she was looking at me and waving like crazy. I looked back, and she pointed toward the ladies' room. I knew that meant that she had to talk to me, so I told Randy that I would be right back and followed her.

"What do you want?" I asked, but before she could answer, girls were pouring into the ladies' room.

"Oh, Jana. It's so exciting," gushed Melanie.

"Yeah," said Alexis. "We're dying to know what's going on."

Suddenly questions were coming at me from all directions, and they were coming so fast that I couldn't answer any of them.

"Did you ask him out, or did he ask you?"

"You can tell he's having a good time. What are you talking about?"

"Did he say if any other boys are going to ask girls out?"

"I have to get back," I said. "Randy's going to wonder what happened to me. I'll tell you all about it later."

I started to leave when I felt a hand on my arm. It was Melanie and she had a dreamy look on her face. "Scott is one of Randy's best friends," she said. "Just think! Maybe he will get the idea and ask me out, too."

I felt like a queen as I hurried back to our table. Usually Taffy was the envy of every girl in the sixth grade, but now it was me. And if any boys asked them out, they would be grateful to me for starting it all. I was so happy I thought I'd die.

Finally Randy and I finished every last crumb of the pizza and drained our Cokes. We even ate all the ice out of the cups. We had been sitting in our booth so long that the place was almost empty. Even Taffy and Mona were gone. The waitress was beginning to give us dirty looks so Randy stood up and said, "I'll pay for this, and then I guess we'd better go."

I nodded and started to follow him when I got this great idea. "I'll be along in a minute," I said. "My sneaker is untied."

Bending over, I undid my perfectly tied left sneaker and retied it as slowly as I could. When I could see that Randy wasn't looking at me I scanned his side of the table for something—anything—that I could take for a souvenir of our very first date. I couldn't take the pizza pan, of course, and his paper napkin was covered with tomato sauce. Then I spotted his straw. That was it. The perfect souvenir. Not only had he drunk his Coke out of that straw, but his lips had touched it. I closed my eyes and imagined touching my lips to the same place. It would be almost like a kiss. Grabbing the straw, I jammed it into the pocket of my jacket before he looked around. I'd die if he saw me. He'd think I was some kind of nut.

My heart was pounding as we left Mama Mia's, and I couldn't help wondering if my face was as red as it felt. If Randy suspected anything, he didn't show it, and we walked home still talking about the things we liked and didn't like.

I couldn't remember ever getting from Mama Mia's to my apartment building so fast, but suddenly we were there. We stood on the step for a couple of minutes, and then he said, "Well, I guess I'd better be going. I'll see you Monday."

I watched him walk down the street thinking that it was true love. I knew that not even Taffy Sinclair could come between us now, and I pulled Randy's straw out of my pocket and put it to my lips.

4 ✿

*T*hat night I slept with Randy's straw under my pillow where I could touch it anytime I wanted to. I had called my friends right away since they were dying to know all about my date, but I didn't tell them about my souvenir. I felt a little guilty, but it was just too private to tell anyone about, even my four very best friends in the world.

All weekend I tried to practice what I would say to Randy when I saw him at school on Monday, but nothing sounded right. Even though we had a lot in common, I couldn't just walk up to him and start talking about deep-dish pepperoni, green pepper, and mushroom pizza or about watching fireworks on the Fourth of July. I would have to wait and see what he said first.

As it turned out, he didn't say anything. When my friends and I got to the school ground, Randy was out on the ball field tossing around a football with Scott Daly and Mark Peters. I was sure that any minute he would look in my direction, and then when he saw me he would wave and maybe even come over to talk to me. But he didn't even look my way. He didn't wave, and he certainly didn't come over to talk to me. He just kept right on tossing that stupid football back and forth as if it were the most important thing in the world. My heart sank into my shoes. Had he forgotten about all the things we had in common already?

"He's probably telling Mark and Scott all about your great date," Christie offered hopefully.

"Or maybe he's just shy," said Melanie.

"Don't worry about Randy right now," said Beth. "Look who's coming."

I looked, and I thought I'd die. It was Curtis Trowbridge, and he was waving and running toward us. "Hey, guys. Guess what?" he shouted. He was practically breathless when he stopped beside us. "You'll never guess what Wiggins is cooking up. You're going to love it.

Curtis looked really excited. I knew that there was no way to get rid of him now. "So what's your big news?" I asked.

"Yeah, Curtis. What is it this time?" asked Beth in a bored voice. Curtis was always coming up with something that he thought was big news.

"Sorry. I'd love to tell you, but I can't." Curtis cocked his head to one side and winked at me. "Actually, nobody is supposed to know about it, but a good newspaperman is always on top of the news."

"So how did you find out this huge secret?" I challenged.

"A good newspaperman always protects his sources."

I started to ask him if his source was a water fountain since he got most of his big news by hanging around the water fountain in front of the office and eavesdropping on the teachers talking to Mrs. Winchell, the principal, but I didn't. I just shrugged, and my friends and I left him standing there and headed for the door.

The first bell rang just as we got to our lockers. I threw my jacket on the hook inside the door and grabbed my books off the shelf. Just as I slammed my locker door and started toward the classroom I saw something that made me stop. It was Randy, and he was coming up the hall with Mark and Scott. It was the perfect chance. I was sure that Randy hadn't said anything to me on the school ground because he and his friends had been too busy tossing the football around. And besides, they were too far away. But now he would have to walk right past me to get to class. I told my friends to go on inside, and I leaned against the door to Wiggins's room and pretended to be looking for something in my notebook.

Out of the corner of my eye I could see three pairs of sneakers coming closer as I flipped notebook pages.

My heart was pounding. I had it all planned. I would look up, act surprised to see him, and give him a big smile. Then he would turn those gorgeous brown eyes toward me and flash his 1,000-watt smile.

"Hey, Randy. Look who's waiting for you." It was Joel Murphy, and he and Keith Masterson had come up behind Randy and Mark and Scott.

"Yeah, Randy," teased Keith. "It's Jana Banana. Your girlfriend! Randy Kirwan's got a girlfriend."

"Lay off, guys," said Mark.

Joel and Keith grabbed each other and faked kissing, making loud smooching noises. I was so embarrassed I thought I'd die. Joel and Keith were doubling over with laughter. I didn't know what Randy was doing. I couldn't look anymore.

I slammed my notebook shut and raced into the room, sliding into my seat as fast as I could. Jana Banana! I hated that name. I stared straight ahead as the room filled up. I didn't dare look at Randy or else somebody might start teasing him. Or even worse, they might call me Jana Banana in front of the class.

Boys are such jerks, I thought. Especially sixth-grade boys. Only Randy was different, but what could he do with two total jerks for friends?

I had forgotten all about Curtis's big news, but the class had barely gotten started when Wiggins stood beside her desk and held her hand up for silence the way she always did when she was about to make a big announcement. Wiggins is short for Winifred Wiggins, and she's been teaching sixth grade ever since the school building was built right after the Korean War. Nobody knows how old she is, but she seems pretty old. I think it's a wonder that she's still alive. Anyway, there she stood with her red curls bobbing and her eyes positively sparkling behind her wire-framed glasses.

"Class!" she said, punching the air with her index finger for emphasis. "We are going to begin a unit on computers. As I'm sure most of you know, computers are becoming bigger and bigger parts of our everyday lives. Some of you may already have computers at home."

A bunch of kids raised their hands and waved them around to show off that they already had home computers. I sighed and threw a dirty look at the back of Curtis Trowbridge's head. If this was the exciting surprise that Wiggins was cooking up, it was pretty boring. But Wiggins wasn't through with us yet.

"Before we start learning computer literacy and practicing on the machines in the Media Center, we are going to do a little experiment that will be a lot of fun and will also help you understand just how computers work."

"For this experiment, you will each fill out a questionnaire about things you like and dislike. Then I will feed your answers into the big computer in the principal's office. This afternoon, right after lunch, you will each get a personal reply from the computer. It will tell you which boy and which girl in this class you have the most things in common with. I guarantee that there will be some surprises, and I know you'll all have a lot of fun."

My eyes opened wide. I was thinking about those computer dating places where they find the person you have a lot in common with and arrange a date for you. That was how they did it, wasn't it? They gave you a questionnaire to fill out and then fed it into their computer to find out who you matched up with. In one advertisement I saw in a magazine they had even called the computer a "Romance Machine." It was too fabulous to be true. Good old Wiggins. Because of her, both my questionnaire and Randy's would go into the machine, and then the whole world would know how perfect we were for each other.

Wiggins was going on and on about computers and how they worked, and I tried to listen. But mostly all I could think about was Randy and our date. I wondered if he was thinking about me, too, but I was still afraid to look at him.

The questions on the sheets Wiggins sent down each row were fill in the blank, with the blank being what you liked or disliked. I tried to listen as she explained how that made it easier for the computer to compare answers. I knew I had to concentrate on what I was doing. If I goofed, it could mean disaster. I looked at the first question. WHAT IS YOUR FAVORITE FOOD?

That was easy. Deep-dish pepperoni, green pepper, and mushroom pizza. I started to write that down, but then I stopped. Randy had said that was his favorite kind of pizza, but was it his absolutely favorite kind of food? Maybe he was a fried chicken nut. Or maybe his favorite food in the whole world was something weird like liverwurst or oxtail soup. I decided to skip that one for now and come back to it later.

Next came another "What do you like best" question. WHAT SPORT DO YOU LIKE BEST? Up until last weekend I would have probably answered "bicycling," since I love to ride my bike, or "swimming," since I like to go to the beach in the summertime. But things were different now that Randy had asked me to watch his football game. Surely football was his favorite sport, so I wrote "FOOTBALL" in large letters.

The rest was about the same. Even on the other side of the paper, the "Like the Least" questions were pretty standard stuff. Still, I couldn't help thinking that I didn't really know very much about Randy. I had been so sure that we had tons of things in common, but now that I had to fill out this questionnaire, I wasn't sure anymore.

As I looked back over the questions, I tried to figure out how he would answer them. Under "Like the Least" I had just naturally put "Dust the house." But what would Randy say? He had probably never dusted the house in his life. Maybe I should change it to "Take out the garbage" or "Mow the lawn," I thought, even though I live in an apartment and don't have a lawn to mow. Randy has a lawn, and it's probably his job to mow it. I was getting confused. This was a lot harder than I had imagined it would be.

Finally I settled on "Take out the garbage" for the chore I liked the least, and I put "Deep-dish pepperoni, green pepper, and mushroom pizza" for the food I liked best. I was thinking about some of the other ones that might need changing when Wiggins held up her hand again.

"Time's up," she said. "Pass all the papers forward. You'll get the results after lunch."

Waiting for afternoon and the results would be like waiting for Christmas. It would take forever to come. And when it did and we got the results back, what if I found out that Randy and I didn't have enough things in common after all? What if we each matched up with someone else? My heart dropped into my shoes. What if he matched up with Taffy Sinclair?

No, I thought. Randy and I were meant for each other, and the Romance Machine was going to prove it.

5 ✻

"If I don't match up with Scott Daly I'll just die!" said Melanie. "I know he likes me. You should see how he acts when no one is looking, and he's always borrowing notebook paper and pencils."

We were sitting in the cafeteria having lunch, and all anyone could talk about was the computer matchup.

"If only Mr. Scott had filled out a questionnaire," Christie murmured. "I just know we would match up." Christie's mother, Mrs. Winchell, is principal of Mark Twain Elementary, and Mr. Scott is the new assistant principal this year. Christie has had a crush on him ever since the beginning of school.

"It wouldn't make any difference if he had filled out a questionnaire," said Katie. "It's all very scientific. The computer matches up people according to what they have in common. What could you and Mr. Scott possibly have in common?"

Christie looked positively stricken. Katie ignored the expression on her face and went right on talking, making things worse with every word she said.

"Just because you like someone doesn't mean that you have anything in common. It might just be a physical attraction. And don't forget. Wiggins said that there would be lots of surprises. Who knows, maybe all of us have picked the wrong friends. Maybe we don't even know that there is someone else in our class that we should be hanging out with."

"There won't be any surprises for me," I said confidently. "At least not when it comes to boys. Randy and I talked about all the things we like and don't like at Mama Mia's before we even knew there would be any questionnaires. You would never believe how much *we* have in common."

Nobody said anything for the next few minutes. I couldn't help thinking about my four best friends as I finished my lunch. Melanie might match up with Scott since she watches every move he makes and probably knows everything he likes and dislikes. But what about the other three? Beth never acts as if she knows boys are alive, and Christie only thinks about Mr. Scott. But Katie is the worst. She practically hates boys.

I also couldn't help thinking about my parents. If there had been computers in those days and my mother and father had done a matchup, maybe they would never have gotten together. I was sure my father wasn't an alcoholic when my mother first met him—she would never have gone out with someone like that—but still, for things to turn out the way they did with the divorce and everything, there must have been a lot of differences between them. In fact, from what I knew about both of them, I couldn't think of a single thing they had in common. Except for me, of course. *Good grief!* I thought. If they had done a computer matchup, I might never have been born.

I decided not to think about that anymore. It was too depressing. Besides, I could hardly wait to get to class. I wondered if Wiggins planned to torture us by making us wait half the afternoon to give out our computer printouts. Still, she had said after lunch.

Sure enough, she called the class to order and then read practically a million announcements. I tapped the eraser of my pencil on the edge of my desk and tried to listen, but all I could think about was the Romance Machine and the matchup. I could hardly wait to get the results. I needed them to prove to Joel and Keith and everybody else that Randy and I were meant for each other and that our romance was nothing to joke about. I wasn't the only one who was antsy, though. All over the room kids were squirming in their seats.

"Attention please!" said Wiggins. She was using her general's voice, which meant that she had noticed how antsy everyone was, and she had picked up a stack of green and white striped papers off of her desk.

She cleared her throat. "All right, boys and girls. The moment has arrived for each of you to find out which boy and which girl in this class you have the most in common with. I will give you exactly five minutes to talk among yourselves and compare results. BUT," she raised her finger into the air like an exclamation point, "remember that these answers are completely confidential, and it is entirely up to you to decide whether you want to tell anyone who you matched up with."

Everybody was squirming again. I looked at my four best friends, exchanging nervous looks with each one of them and thinking that a person would have to match up with someone pretty drippy to keep it a secret from everyone.

Wiggins was walking up and down the rows handing out folded papers with names on the front of them. Twice she stopped near me, and both times I almost grabbed the paper out of her hand as it shot by me and went to someone sitting close by. I could hear kids giggling and whispering as more and more of them read their matchups. I was beginning to worry. Where was mine? Had my questionnaire gotten lost?

Finally Wiggins handed me a folded paper with my name on it. I held my breath. What if I didn't get Randy's name? What if I got someone weird like Curtis Trowbridge or Clarence Marshall? My hands were shaking as I opened the paper. I squinted my eyes almost shut and looked out through the slits at the two names:

BETH BARRY AND RANDY KIRWAN

I nearly collapsed with relief. I had been right all along. I knew that Randy and I had a lot of things in common. Now the Romance Machine had proved it. And best of all, now everybody would know it.

"Psst. Jana. Who did you get?"

It was Beth. I didn't even try to control the smile that spread over my face. "You," I said, "and you know who." I nodded toward Randy. I didn't have the nerve to look at him yet. "Who did you get?"

Instead of Beth, I heard another voice coming from the other side of me. "I got Randy Kirwan," gushed Alexis Duvall.

"Me, too."

"I got Randy's name."

It was as if there were an echo in the room. A few girls, like Melanie, were saying other boys' names, but girls all over the room were saying that they got Randy Kirwan. I sat there in shock. How could a thing like that happen? There must be a mistake. I had Randy's name, and surely he had mine. I sneaked a look at him out of the corner of my eye. His face was as red as fire.

"Hey, Jana. I got your name. Whose name did you get?"

It was Curtis Trowbridge. I pretended that I hadn't heard him. It was bad enough that he got my name, but why did he have to say it out loud in front of the whole sixth grade?

"Hey, Jana. I said that I got your name," said Curtis.

Taffy Sinclair turned around and gave me an icy smile. I could tell she was glad that Curtis was making an idiot of me. "I got Randy Kirwan, too," she said.

I felt hot all over. I wouldn't have been surprised if I had started breathing fire and smoke. How dare Taffy Sinclair say that she had Randy's name. She couldn't. Randy didn't care about her. He cared about me. Well, I would show her a thing or two. I'd show everybody.

"Whose name did you get, Randy?" I challenged, still ignoring Curtis Trowbridge.

"He probably got Jana Banana's name," said Joel Murphy. He was looking at me and laughing as if he thought getting my name was some kind of joke.

"Yeah. Jana Banana," taunted Keith Masterson. "She's his girlfriend."

Randy looked down at the paper in his hand. It was easy to see that he was still embarrassed, and I knew Taffy Sinclair had a lot to do with it. He started to say something, but then he stopped.

Come on, I thought. Tell her. Tell everybody that you got my name.

"Oh, come on, Randy," pleaded Beth. "Tell us who you got."

There was a chorus of "Yeah," "Come on!" and "Tell us whose name you got."

Kids were milling around talking and laughing and a few were whispering "Jana Banana." My ears were getting so hot that they felt as if they would melt any minute. Why didn't Randy just say whose name he got and get it over with?

The room got quiet as Randy started folding his green and white striped paper. He did it slowly, and you could tell that he was thinking the situation over. He folded the paper into smaller and smaller squares until it was just about the size of a grape.

Then he looked up and said in a quiet voice, "Miss Wiggins said that nobody has to tell." With that he stuffed the grape-size paper into the pocket of his jeans.

"I'm not going to tell either," shouted Scott Daly.

"Me, either," said Mark Peters. "If Randy won't tell, I'm not going to either."

"I got Jana Morgan," offered Curtis.

"Well, I'm not going to tell whose name I got," said Clarence Marshall. "Girls. Yuk!" He put his hands around his neck and faked throwing up. "Who needs them?"

Suddenly every boy in the whole class, except Curtis Trowbridge and Randy, was shouting that he wasn't going to tell whose name he got in the girl matchup and faking throwing up like Clarence. And every girl in the class was glaring at me as if it were all my fault.

6 ✻

At that moment I felt as if a trap door had opened up under my feet and I had dropped into the pits. The dismal pits. I couldn't believe that Randy would let me down like that. But the looks on all the girls' faces had me convinced that I had more than just Randy Kirwan to worry about.

Melanie dropped to one knee beside my desk. She was frowning and she said in a loud whisper, "Now look what you did, Jana. I may never find out if Scott got my name."

I threw her a poison-dart look. "Don't blame me. I had nothing to do with it."

"Oh, yeah? You had a date with Randy Saturday, didn't you? And you were the one Joel and Keith were teasing him about, aren't you?"

"So?"

"Figure it out," she said. "If they were teasing him about you after the date, just think how they would tease him if he got your name."

I didn't answer. If Randy really liked me, it shouldn't matter if they teased him. Sixth-grade boys were always teasing somebody about something. It was a dumb conversation anyway. I couldn't see how anybody could think it was my fault that Randy Kirwan wouldn't tell whose name he got for the girl matchup. And I certainly didn't have anything to do with all the other boys deciding not to tell either. But that didn't stop the girls from being mad at me.

Unfortunately, that was only part of my troubles. I didn't know it at first, but this whole computer matchup was going to turn into a disaster. It took Wiggins a while to restore order. In the meantime, I got some more news. None of it good.

1. Not only had Taffy Sinclair gotten Randy's name, but nine out of fourteen girls in the sixth grade got him as their boy matchup, *including* Beth Barry. It was bad enough that he was so popular that practically everybody had a crush on him, but my best friend in the world! I couldn't believe it. She had always acted as if she didn't know that boys were on the face of the earth, and all along she had a secret crush on Randy.

2. Melanie and Taffy Sinclair got each other's names. Melanie pretended to be mad, but I saw her watching Taffy out of the corner of her eye. Now that she was

getting thin and a lot prettier, was she going to turn into someone stuck-up and snotty like Taffy Sinclair?

3. Christie refused to speak to any of us for the rest of the day because no one in The Fabulous Five got her name. She said that proved that we all just pretended to be her friend because her mother is principal of our school. She said we thought that gave us special privileges, which is a big fat lie!

4. Katie was mad, too. Even though she says that she doesn't like boys, she was upset when her boy matchup said "Computer error #14" and she read it out loud and the whole class laughed.

5. And then there was good old Curtis Trowbridge. You can always count on him to make a bad thing worse. Why did he have to be the only boy who would tell who he matched up with? All afternoon he tore around yelling, "I got Jana Morgan! I got Jana Morgan!" to anyone who would listen.

In fact, it turned out to be a terrible day, after all. In addition to all the girls being mad at me, practically everybody in the whole sixth grade was mad at everybody else. During afternoon recess lots of kids weren't going around with their regular friends. Christie stood all by herself near the swings and kept giving the rest of us poison-dart looks. I walked around with Melanie and Beth and Katie, but I made sure to stay as far away from Beth as I could. I couldn't forget that she was a traitor.

If that was the dismal pits, then I don't know how to describe what happened next. We were still outside for recess, and I had noticed that Taffy Sinclair was with a group of girls that she doesn't usually go around with. Of course Mona Vaughn was there, but so was Alexis Duvall and Lisa Snow and Kim Baxter. It looked like a meeting of the Randy Kirwan fan club.

Anyway, they were whispering and looking at me. Then suddenly they started giggling. I could feel my ears getting hot. I didn't know what they were giggling about, but I was sure that it was something pretty terrible and that it was about me.

Taffy stopped giggling. Then she looked straight at me and said in a voice so loud that just about everybody on the playground could hear, "If Randy had Jana's name, he would have said so since he had a date with her." She paused for a minute to be dramatic and then gave me a wicked smile and said, "Obviously he has someone else's name."

She might as well have added, "It must be mine," because from the tone of her voice you could tell that was what she meant.

I thought I would explode. It was bad enough that she would say such a thing, but how could Alexis and Lisa and Kim be on her side? I looked around quickly to see if Randy had heard what she had said, but he was too far away. At least that much was going my way.

The rest of the day I had trouble concentrating on what Wiggins was talking about in class. My mind was on Randy. He didn't look at me once. I tried not to look at him, but I couldn't help it. Even when I wasn't looking at him, I kept seeing him with that green and white striped printout in his hand saying that his matchup was a secret. Why would he do a thing like that to me? He had always been such a kind and sensitive person. Was Taffy right? Did Randy have someone else's name? Did he have hers?

I could hardly wait to get home after school. I wanted to be alone so that I could do some more thinking and maybe figure everything out. But wouldn't you know it. Mom was there. She said that she had left work early because she was coming down with the flu. I had to admit that she looked terrible. She was on the sofa all bundled up in a blanket. Her nose was red and her eyes watery and her voice sounded scratchy.

I put my books in my room and went back to the living room to see if she needed anything. "Just some company," she said. "Sit down for a minute and tell me about your day."

I sat beside her and immediately looked down at my feet. The computer matchup had been the biggest thing in my day, and I didn't want to talk about it. Not even to Mom. It was just too humiliating.

"Things didn't go so well, huh?" she said gently.

"Worse than that." I hesitated as long as I could, but if I couldn't talk to Mom about it, who could I talk to? Finally I broke down and told her about the matchup. I started by telling her about Christie being mad at all of us and about Melanie and Taffy getting each other and about Katie getting "Computer error #14" for her boy matchup. Mom chuckled at that, and then I told her how mad I was at Beth. "She knows how much I like Randy Kirwan," I said. "And all along she's liked him, too."

Mom didn't say anything for a minute. She just gave me a sympathetic look. I guess she was waiting for me to cool off. Finally she said, "You haven't said anything about who Randy matched up with. Was that a surprise, too?"

There was such a big lump in my throat that at first I just nodded. Then I shook my head. Finally I sputtered, "I don't know. Nine out of fourteen girls in our class got his name, but he wouldn't tell anybody whose name he got. I've never been so embarrassed in my life."

"Did he say why?"

I shook my head. "Melanie said it's because Joel Murphy and Keith Masterson were teasing him about me. But I can't believe that's it. I know Randy likes me. That's only part of it though. Wiggins said that nobody had to tell if they didn't want to, and when Randy wouldn't, then none of the other boys would either— except Curtis Trowbridge. Now all the girls say it's my fault that none of the boys will tell, and they're mad at me. It wasn't my fault, Mom, honest. I just wish I knew why *he* won't tell."

Mom got a sad look on her face, and even though she had a cold, she pulled me close and gave me a hug.

"Maybe Randy is feeling a little bit self-conscious about things. Being the first boy to have a date with a girl. Being teased by the other boys. And now matching up with over half the girls in his class. Randy is such a nice person that maybe he doesn't want to hurt any of their feelings. I don't know if that's it either, sweetheart. I wish I did. I wish I had all the answers for you and could make you feel better."

Even though she didn't have the answers, sitting there with her arms around me made me feel a little better. I might have stayed there forever except that just then the doorbell rang. We exchanged surprised looks. "Who on earth could that be?" she said.

I jumped up and raced for the door. "I'll get it." What if it was Randy? What if he had come over to tell me that he really did get my name after all and that now he was ready to tell? What if he said he hadn't told in school because he wanted to tell me in private? Maybe I had been wrong to be so worried. I plastered a smile on my face and threw open the door.

"Hello." A pretty young woman was standing there. She was carrying a huge bouquet of flowers. "Is this the Morgan residence?"

My heart skipped a beat and I nodded and stared at the flowers. They were chrysanthemums in beautiful fall shades of yellow and bronze.

"I'm from Blossom Time Florist, and these are for Mrs. Patricia Morgan."

"That's my mom," I said in a voice just barely above a whisper. "I'll take them."

After the lady from Blossom Time Florist left I just stood there holding the flowers and staring at the door. I had been so sure that it would be Randy, but it wasn't. I wanted to cry.

"Who is it, Jana?" Mom called. "Did I hear my name?"

"These are for you," I said. Then I marched back to the sofa, handing her the bouquet as if it were made of snakes instead of flowers.

"I'll bet I know who they're from." She opened the card and nodded. "Pink. Just as I thought. I've only been home for a couple of hours and he's already sending me get well flowers." Mom sighed and gave me a look that was a mixture of amusement and exasperation. "I don't know what I'm going to do with that man. Ever since he asked me to marry him and I told him I needed time to think about it, he won't leave me alone for a minute."

I mumbled something about doing my homework and went to my room. I closed the door behind me and sat down on the bed, pulling Randy's straw out from its hiding place under my pillow. I just sat there staring at it for a long time thinking about Mom and Pink and the beautiful flowers and trying to figure out what she was doing right that I was doing wrong.

7 ❊

Mom was still sick the next morning. She came scuffing out of her bedroom wearing her warmest robe and fur-lined slippers. She blew her nose loudly and said that she was staying home from work. Then she mumbled something about how I should "hab a dice day" and went back to bed again. I was awfully sorry that Mom was sick, but I had to admit that her not being around when I got ready for school couldn't have come at a better time.

I hurried through breakfast and then raced to my closet to pick out something special to wear. It wasn't that I was trying to impress anyone, especially not Randy Kirwan. I just felt like getting a little more dressed up than usual. Besides, I got tired of wearing the same old things all the time. My new blue plaid skirt almost jumped off the hanger at me. It even had a matching sweater. Mom said that it made me look a lot older and that I should save it for special occasions, but I didn't think it would hurt to wear it to school just this one time.

When I was dressed I went into the bathroom and opened the drawer where she keeps her makeup. I did it very slowly so that the drawer wouldn't squeak and wake her up. I had been reading in teen magazines that makeup would help accent a person's best features. I had explained that to Mom, but she is awfully old-fashioned about some things. Anyway, my eyes are my best feature so I spread some blue eye shadow over my lids and brushed her darkest mascara on my lashes. That was better. I decided to add some lip gloss and a little blusher, and when I was finished I looked so much better that I almost wished Mom could see me.

Putting on makeup had taken extra time, and when I got to school the playground was crowded with kids. I stopped outside the gate for a minute wishing that I had a mirror so that I could check myself over one more time. I must have been daydreaming because I suddenly realized that Katie Shannon was standing in front of me making a terrible face.

"Jana Morgan, what have you done to yourself?" she shrieked.

Leave it to Katie, I thought. "What do you mean, what have I done to myself? I've just fixed up a little. That's all."

"Fixed up," she scoffed. "You look like a clown. I think this must be circus day. There are clowns all over the playground."

Surprised, I looked around. At first I couldn't figure out what she was talking about. The playground looked pretty ordinary, with groups of kids standing around waiting for the first bell to ring. Then I glanced toward the side of the building where the sixth-graders usually congregate. Alexis Duvall and Lisa Snow were standing together talking. They both looked as if they were going to a party. Alexis had her light brown hair piled on top of her head. Lisa was wearing long dangling earrings, and they both had on heels. As I got closer I could see that they were wearing makeup too.

"Just wait until you see Kim Baxter," said Katie. "She must have put her makeup on while she rode the school bus—at the same time they went over a bunch of potholes. It's smeared all over her face. What's the matter with everybody today, anyway?"

I didn't answer. I just kept looking around. Katie was right. Practically every girl in sixth grade was dressed up, and most of them had on tons of makeup. I was looking for Taffy Sinclair when I noticed girls rushing over toward the bicycle racks. It was practically a stampede. They were zeroing in from all directions. I didn't understand why until I heard Sara Sawyer say in an icky sweet voice, "Hi, Randy."

Randy locked his bike to the rack and glanced around. He looked surprised, but before he could say anything Alexis Duvall marched right up to him. She was waving a paper in her hand. "Here's your math homework, Randy," she gushed. "It must have blown out of your book. I SAVED IT FOR YOU."

I felt as if I was going to throw up. Sara and Alexis were flirting with him. Didn't they know how silly they looked? Did they really think Randy Kirwan would fall for a thing like that? I looked at Katie and she looked back at me. I could tell she felt the same way I did.

"Thanks, Alexis," said Randy. He was grinning like crazy. "I would have gotten into a lot of trouble without my homework."

"She probably snitched it out of his book when he wasn't looking," I muttered. "She probably . . ."

I felt Katie's hand on my arm, and before I could finish my sentence she interrupted me. "Look! Will you get a load of Taffy Sinclair."

I did. And then I blinked a couple of times in case I was seeing things. It was Taffy Sinclair, all right, and she was walking with Melanie Edwards. They were heading straight for Randy and the crowd of girls around him. Taffy was batting her eyes and smiling her fake smile, but that wasn't all. She had on makeup, too, and she was running a brush through her long blond hair so that everybody would notice her new curly perm.

Randy certainly noticed. His eyes nearly popped out of their sockets.

"Hi, Randy," Taffy cooed, flipping her new curls over one shoulder. "Could I talk to you for a minute?"

Then she stepped away from Melanie as if she had something private to talk to him about.

"Sure, Taffy."

Randy almost tripped over his feet getting to her. It was disgusting. Taffy and Randy are just about the same height, but somehow Taffy managed to scrunch down so that she was looking up at him with her big blue eyes. Then she reached out and put a hand very lightly on his arm and began saying something in such a soft voice that I couldn't hear even though I strained as hard as I could. Apparently Randy couldn't hear her either because he moved closer. Suddenly he looked at her and smiled. I thought I'd die. It was the same 1,000-watt smile that he always gave me. Was he telling her that she was the one he matched up with? I could feel my heart breaking into a million tiny pieces.

"That's men for you," said Katie. She must have seen the look on my face.

"I don't know what's happened to him," I said. "We had such a great time Saturday, and we have so much in common. I can't believe he didn't get my name in the computer matchup. Why is he acting this way?"

"Did you just get in from outer space or what, Jana Morgan? Did you ever hear of the word *conceit*?"

I frowned at Katie. "Randy Kirwan is not conceited," I insisted. "He's kind and sensitive . . ."

"And handsome and popular and has practically every girl in sixth grade falling all over him including

Taffy Sinclair. What do you mean he isn't conceited? You must be blind."

What did Katie know about boys, anyway? She didn't even like boys, and what's more, they didn't like her either.

"Well, I certainly don't need any advice from you!" I cried and stormed off toward the school. I opened my locker wishing I could crawl inside and hide there until time to go home. I had never been so miserable in my life. I had thought that the computer matchup would turn out to be fun and that everyone would find out that Randy Kirwan and I were meant for each other. Some romance machine it had turned out to be. Instead, my life was a disaster. Every girl in the sixth grade was mad at me for something that wasn't my fault. I was mad at Beth for having a secret crush on Randy when she knew all along that I liked him. Christie wasn't speaking to me because I didn't match up with her. Melanie had matched up with Taffy and was getting friendly with her and probably turning into a snotty and stuck-up person. And I had just yelled at Katie and made enemies with her.

Worst of all, I had just found out that the most wonderful boy in the world wasn't as wonderful as I thought. As much as it hurt to do it, I had to face the truth. Randy Kirwan was conceited.

8 ✽

I stood there for a long time staring into my locker as if I expected the answer to all my problems to come tumbling off the shelf and land at my feet. It didn't. Behind me the hallway was getting noisy as kids slammed their lockers and shouted to each other. I didn't pay any attention until I heard Melanie's voice.

"Gosh, I love your perm. It looks terrific. How do you think I'd look with my hair curled?"

Naturally it was Taffy Sinclair who answered her. She must have known I was listening because her voice was really loud.

"Oh, Mel. It would be darling," she gushed. "I think you'd love it, and boys really like girls with curly hair."

54

"They do? Then maybe I will get a perm. Only I'm not sure if I'd know how to style it once I got it."

"Meet me in the girls' bathroom right after lunch, and I'll show you some different ways you could wear it."

"Okay. I'll meet you after lunch."

"Great, Mel."

By the time I turned around they had both disappeared into the classroom. "Great, Mel," I mimicked under my breath. Mel! I thought. It sounded like a boy's name. Or a dog. I giggled. Maybe Melanie was going to become Taffy's pet dog. I could hear it all now. HERE, MEL. COME ON, GIRL. ROLL OVER. I sank into my seat still daydreaming about Melanie, complete with dog tag and leash, following Taffy through the halls of Mark Twain Elementary.

Wiggins threw a fit when she saw all the makeup, and she made us go to the girls' bathroom two by two to wash it off. I held my breath, wondering who she would send with me.

"Jana Morgan and Taffy Sinclair. You may go now."

I couldn't believe it. Not Taffy Sinclair. How could Wiggins do a thing like this to me? Didn't I have enough problems already?

I left my seat and headed for the door. I could tell without looking that everybody in the whole class was staring at me. Me and Taffy Sinclair. There was not one person in that room who didn't know how much we hate each other. I thought I heard someone giggle—probably Mona Vaughn—but I didn't look around.

Taffy sits near the front of the room so that she can make brownie points with the teacher, which is why she got to the door first. We didn't look at each other as we started down the hall. Once I peeked out of the corner of my eye at her. She was prancing along with her nose stuck up in the air.

We had just gotten into the girls' bathroom when she looked at me in the mirror and gave me a nasty smile. "I know something you don't know," she said.

I didn't answer. I just stood there staring at her as she wet a paper towel, squirted some smelly green soap on it, and started to wash her face. I knew it had something to do with Randy Kirwan.

"You think you are so smart. You think Randy Kirwan got your name in the matchup, but he didn't."

I could feel little explosions going off in my heart. How dare Taffy Sinclair say a thing like that? "You don't know what you're talking about," I growled.

Taffy pretended not to hear what I said. She just went on scrubbing her face and smiling her nasty smile. "Can't you figure it out for yourself? Since you and Randy had a date Saturday after the football game, if he had your name he would tell. Since he won't tell, that proves that he has someone else's name."

"You don't really believe a crazy thing like that, do you?" I challenged.

"Of course," said Taffy. "And so does everybody else. What other reason would he have for refusing to tell?"

I shot a poison-dart look her way. "Maybe he's tired of being teased about me."

"Ha! Why would he care if kids tease him? He's only keeping his girl matchup a secret because he feels *sorry* for you and doesn't want to hurt your feelings. Oh, well. It doesn't matter what you think. If he doesn't ask you to go for pizza again after the game this Saturday, it will prove to you and everybody else that I'm right. He doesn't have your name."

I hadn't even thought about the game Saturday afternoon or whether Randy would take me to Mama Mia's again or not. But now Taffy's words echoed in my mind. *If he doesn't ask you to go for pizza again after the game this Saturday, it will prove to you and everybody else that I'm right. He doesn't have your name.* I wanted to scream at Taffy and tell her that she was lying. But I couldn't. I wanted to look her straight in the eye and tell her that Randy *did* have my name and that he *would* ask me to go for pizza again. But what if he didn't? What if Taffy Sinclair was right? She had said that maybe he felt sorry for me and didn't want to hurt my feelings. Hadn't Mom said something about Randy being so nice that maybe he wasn't telling who he matched up with because he didn't want to hurt anyone's feelings? I had never thought about that "anyone" being me. I grabbed a paper towel, held it under the water faucet and scrubbed my face so hard that it hurt.

After I finished washing my face, I didn't wait for Taffy. She was still standing in front of the mirror brushing her new curly perm. I hurried out of that bathroom and stomped down the hall promising myself that I'd show Taffy Sinclair how wrong she was. I'd find a way to get Randy to admit that he had my name if it was the last thing I ever did.

Wiggins gave the class free-reading time while we waited for all the girls with makeup on to go to the bathroom. I propped a book up in front of me and pretended to be reading it. What I needed was a plan, but no matter how hard I tried, I couldn't come up with one for the life of me.

When everybody got back to the room, Wiggins held her hand up for silence. "Today is our big day. We are going to the Media Center this morning to begin working on the computers."

Her smile was so big you would have thought she had just announced that school was canceled for the rest of the year. I groaned. Computers had gotten me into the mess I was in. More computers could only mean more trouble.

She lined us up in twos to march to the Media Center. I looked over to the other side of the room toward Randy's desk just in time to see two girls, Sarah Sawyer and Lisa Snow, almost knock each other down to get close to him. Those show-offs, I thought. Then I smiled with satisfaction as Wiggins motioned for Mark Peters to march with Randy.

When we got to the Media Center, Wiggins led us to the end of the room where the six new computers sat on library tables and told us to sit down on the floor in a large semicircle. She got out a big cardboard illustration of the screen and the computer keyboard and her long pointer and began explaining the various parts and what they were for. Then she went to one of the real computers and demonstrated how to start it up and call up a certain program and how to shut the whole thing down again. I tried to pay attention but I couldn't.

"Now, boys and girls," said Wiggins. "You are finally going to get the chance to use the computers yourselves. But remember one thing. Never, never leave the computer without shutting it down completely. This is very important. Do you think you can all remember that?" Everybody nodded. Then she called up the first six kids to work on the computers. Randy was one of them.

Wiggins handed out work sheets to the rest of us. She said that they would help us remember what she had said while we waited for our turn. I wrote my name at the top of my work sheet and glanced at Randy again. I just couldn't seem to keep my eyes off of him. He looked so handsome sitting in front of his computer punching on the keyboard and then looking at the screen and then back at the keyboard again. I must have been staring at him longer than I realized because suddenly Wiggins was announcing that the next group of six students should come to the computers. When she counted them off, I was number four.

I sat down in front of my computer wishing that I had paid more attention to Wiggins's demonstration. The keyboard looked pretty much like a typewriter and the screen looked like a little television, but beyond that, I was lost.

"Does everybody remember where to find the little switch that turns the computer on?" asked Wiggins. She was standing beside the cardboard illustration again holding her pointer.

Practically everybody shook their head so she pointed to the right place on the computer. I turned on the switch and the computer began to hum.

"And does everybody remember how to call up a program?" she asked. Again, almost nobody did.

Finally a list of questions appeared on the screen. Each multiple choice question had three possible answers with little boxes at the end of each choice. The instructions at the top of the screen said to put an *X* in the correct box and then push Enter. The computer would say if the answer was right or wrong.

I took a deep breath and looked at the first question. It was the same as the first question on the work sheet. I felt better. Maybe this wouldn't be too hard after all. Then I remembered that I hadn't paid much attention to Wiggins because I was too busy thinking about Randy, and I hadn't answered a single question on the work sheet either.

Question 1 said, The cursor always tells you: a. Where the next character will be displayed, b. When you've made a typing error, c. How to get to the cafeteria. I had to laugh at choice *c*. Obviously that was not the right answer, but for the life of me I couldn't remember what Wiggins had said the cursor was really for.

I looked at the other five kids sitting at computers. They were all punching keys on the keyboard as if they knew what they were doing. I looked back at question 1.

Suddenly the air was filled with a piercing sound. My fingers froze on the keyboard. At first I thought someone was screaming, but then I realized that it was the fire alarm. There was instant panic as kids scrambled for the door. Above the noise I heard Wiggins shouting, "Remember, boys and girls. Walk quietly and stay calm."

I started to get up and follow the others, but just then I remembered something else. "Never, never leave the computer without shutting it down completely." My mind was blank. I couldn't remember how I started it up, much less how to shut it down.

"Jana! Come on!"

I looked around. It was Randy, and he was motioning to me. All the other kids had shut down their computers and were heading for the door. I was the only one still standing there. I wanted to run, but my computer was still on.

I can't. I don't know how to shut this thing down, I tried to yell, but suddenly my tongue went numb and I couldn't make a sound. The rest of my body was frozen too, and I just stood there like a statue looking at Randy.

He was still looking at me too, as if he couldn't understand why I didn't come on. I knew in that instant that he didn't feel sorry for me the way Taffy had said. He really cared about me after all. He cared enough to wait for me, to risk his life for me. A picture filled my mind. It was Randy holding my hand and pulling me to safety just as flaming walls crashed behind us. My heart was about to burst with happiness.

All of a sudden Curtis Trowbridge appeared from out of nowhere. He rushed up and started doing something to my computer.

"Don't worry, Jana. I know all about this kind of computer. See. I took care of it for you. It's all shut down."

I couldn't believe it. I looked first at Curtis and then at Randy, who just shrugged and headed out of the room. Then I looked back at Curtis again. He was grinning at me as if he had just done something wonderful. Then Curtis—not Randy—grabbed my arm and pulled me toward the door.

9 ✻

*T*he fire drill was just the beginning of a totally rotten day. Taffy Sinclair had practically every girl in the whole sixth grade giving me dirty looks. I knew what they were thinking. They thought that if Randy didn't ask me for pizza on Saturday, then maybe they would have a chance. In addition to giving me dirty looks, they were all flirting with him like crazy. What was worse, he was flirting back. Every time I looked at him he was talking to a different girl. I thought I'd die.

I was ready to explode by the time I got home from school. I pitched my books down on the sofa and marched into Mom's bedroom.

"You should have seen Randy Kirwan flirting with practically every girl in the sixth grade today," I said.

"He spread himself around like the flu. He is the most conceited boy I ever met."

Mom put down the magazine she was reading and looked at me sympathetically. "I assume that when you say 'practically every girl in the sixth grade,' you mean everybody but you."

"Sort of," I admitted. "You should have seen him though. He talked to Lisa Snow and Beth Barry and Alexis Duvall. And of course, he talked to Taffy Sinclair. And that's not all. When he talked to Mona Vaughn, she got a look on her face as if he had just said that she should be the next Miss America. I couldn't believe it."

"He's certainly getting a lot of special attention from the girls these days. It sounds as if that computer matchup business really went to his head."

"You can say that again," I said.

She didn't. She blew her nose instead, which reminded me that I had been so upset over Randy that I hadn't even asked her how she was feeling.

"How's your cold?" I said. "It's a good thing you stayed in bed all day. It doesn't sound all that great."

"Stayed in bed? Are you kidding? Pink has called every single hour to see how I'm feeling. I've been back and forth between this bed and the phone so many times that I feel as if I've run a marathon."

"Why is he calling so often?"

Mom shrugged. "He just says he's calling to see how I'm feeling and to ask if I need anything. I don't know what's gotten into that man. The flowers yesterday, the phone calls today. But that's not all. He wants to take me to Ricardo's for dinner on Saturday night."

"Ricardo's? Instead of bowling? That's one of the most expensive restaurants in town." I couldn't help being surprised. Pink is an absolute bowling nut, and he and Mom go bowling every single Saturday night.

"You've got it," said Mom. Then she smiled softly and reached for my hand. "It looks as if you and I have the opposite problem."

I nodded and squeezed her hand. I could feel a lump crowd into my throat. She was certainly right about that. She could have Ricardo's. All I wanted was Mama Mia's. I would give anything if Randy Kirwan would pay attention to me the way Pink paid attention to her.

Just then the phone rang. "Pink?" I asked.

Mom looked at her watch and then nodded. "Pink. Do me a favor, will you, honey? Tell him I'm asleep and you don't want to disturb me. I hate to ask you to do that. I know it isn't the truth, but . . ."

"It's okay, Mom. I understand."

I raced into the living room and picked up the receiver. Mom was right. It was Pink.

"Hi, Jana," he said. "I'm just calling to check on your mom. Could I speak to her, please?"

"Gee, Pink. Mom's asleep and I really don't think I should disturb her." I could feel a grin spreading across my face. Lying was fun when you had permission.

"Oh . . . well . . . then could I talk to you for a minute, Jana? There is something that I've been wanting to ask you."

"Sure," I said. He sounded nervous, but I couldn't imagine what he wanted to ask me.

Pink cleared his throat. "I was wondering how you feel about me? What I mean is, I was hoping that you don't have any objection to your mom and me getting married."

I sighed. Mom and I had talked about all of this ages ago. "Of course I like you. You know that. And of course I don't have any objection to you and Mom getting married. Didn't she tell you?"

"Yes, she told me, but I just wanted to make sure."

He paused, but I had the feeling that he wanted to say something else. I was right.

"Can I ask you a favor, Jana? A big favor?"

"Shoot," I said.

"Well, I was wondering if you could . . . you know, sort of talk me up to your mother? I mean, if she knew how much you like me, she might not need so much time to make up her mind. I don't want to sound like I'm pushing her or anything. But I really believe that your mom and I were meant for each other. We really have a lot in common. It might help her realize all of that if she knew you thought so, too."

"Sure, Pink. I'll talk you up," I promised.

I was practically in a trance when I hung up the phone. Two things he said really hit home. *Your mom and*

I were meant for each other. We really have a lot in common.
Those were the same things I had thought all along
about Randy and me. So why was Pink pestering the
living daylights out of Mom and Randy acting as if I
didn't exist? It didn't make sense.

I glanced back in the bedroom at Mom. She was
reading her magazine again. Maybe I shouldn't have
promised Pink that I would talk him up. She acted as if
hearing more about him was the last thing in the world
she wanted. Still, I could see Pink's point. She was only
thinking about him calling all the time instead of his
good qualities. He really did have good qualities. Mom
raved about them all the time when he wasn't driving
her nuts. Maybe reminding her of them wasn't such a
bad idea after all.

My hand was still on the phone when it rang again,
and I almost jumped out of my skin. Was Pink calling
back so soon? He hadn't even given me time to talk to
Mom.

"Hello," I said.

"Hi, Jana." It was Beth.

I frowned. "What do you want?"

"I want to know why you're mad at me."

"Because you're a traitor," I said. "You know that I
like Randy Kirwan, and yet you answered your computer questions so that you would match up with him,
too."

Beth didn't say anything for a minute. What was
there to say? I thought. She was guilty and she knew it.

"Jana Morgan, you know as well as I do that practically every girl in the sixth grade has a crush on Randy. You know that he's the most popular boy in school. So what does popular mean? It means that *everybody* likes him, especially girls."

"So what?" I said. "You're my best friend. At least, you're supposed to be."

"I am your best friend," Beth insisted. "But I couldn't stop liking him just because you liked him, too. Besides," she added slowly, "you don't know for sure that he didn't get your name. You just need to find a way to get him to tell. After all, you're always saying how the two of you have so much in common."

Your mom and I were meant for each other. We really have a lot in common. Suddenly I got this great idea. If it could work for Pink, it just might work for me, too. Maybe this was the plan I had been searching for.

"If you're really my best friend, there is something you could do to help me."

"Okay. What do you want me to do?"

Tingles raced up and down my spine. I took a deep breath and said, "Tomorrow at school you could talk me up to Randy."

10 *

I knew I should go into Mom's room and start talking up Pink, but I didn't. Now that I had a plan to get Randy's attention back, I couldn't think about anything else the whole time I fixed hot dogs for Mom and me for supper. Surely once Randy heard a lot of super things about me, he would get his mind off all those other girls and ask me to go for pizza again. Then once everybody saw us together at Mama Mia's, they would know he had my name and they'd stop listening to Taffy Sinclair.

Still, I couldn't help worrying a little. What if Beth forgot? Or what if she only mentioned me once or twice? Or what if Randy was too busy being conceited and talking to all those other girls to listen? Maybe just one person talking me up wasn't enough. Maybe I needed a whole campaign.

After supper Mom said she was going to take some cold medicine and go right to bed because she couldn't afford to miss another day of work. That meant I could put off talking up Pink until tomorrow. It also meant I had the living room to myself for the entire evening. I smiled. My campaign headquarters, I thought.

I sat down at the end of the sofa by the phone. The next question was, who should I call to help in my campaign? Beth was in already. Christie was the next logical choice, but she was still mad because not one of The Fabulous Five matched up with her. I'd have to think about her. Melanie? Hmmm. She was getting awfully friendly with the enemy. I'd have to think about her, too. Of my very best friends, that only left Katie. How could I ask her to help? She was the one who called Randy "conceited."

I was back to Christie again. Maybe if I asked her to help me with something as important as Randy Kirwan, she would see that I still liked her. It was worth a try.

I crossed and uncrossed my fingers three times for luck and dialed her number. It rang only once.

"Hello."

"Hi, Mrs. Winchell. This is Jana. May I speak to Christie, please?"

"Hello, Jana. Just a moment. I'll see if I can find her."

I held that receiver for ages. I was beginning to wonder if even Mrs. Winchell would come back on. Finally I heard sounds on the other end, and Christie said hello.

"Hi, Christie. What are you doing?" I thought I had better start off with casual conversation and then work up to the big favor I planned to ask.

"I'm washing my hair," she said in a grumpy voice.

I panicked. "Gee, that's great. Not that I noticed how dirty it was at school today or anything. What I mean is . . ."

"What do you want, Jana?"

"I just called to talk," I lied. My pulse was racing. If I goofed up this conversation, she probably wouldn't speak to me for the rest of my life.

"You called to pretend that you're my friend because you want something. Didn't you? Just because my mom's principal of Mark Twain Elementary, you think you can butter me up and get anything you want."

"That's not true, Christie, and you know it," I said.

"Oh, yeah? Prove it."

I could see I wasn't getting anywhere. I certainly couldn't prove anything to her by asking her to do me a favor. Then I got this great idea.

"Forget it," I said, trying to sound as dejected as possible. "You wouldn't believe me no matter what I said or did. Besides, what I really need right now is a good friend to talk to and give me advice. I'd better go and call someone else. Bye."

"Don't hang up yet," Christie said. "What do you mean 'give me advice'?" she asked. Did something bad happen?"

I could tell I had her hooked. It was all I could do to keep from giggling. "Not exactly."

"Come on, Jana. Tell me. What happened?"

"Well . . ."

"Jana!"

I knew I had stalled long enough. "Nothing has really happened. It's just that Randy Kirwan acts as if he has forgotten all about our date and all the things we have in common. He keeps flirting with everybody else as if he doesn't know I'm alive. I was just wondering if you would talk me up when you're around him at school tomorrow."

There was a pause. "I thought you wanted advice, not a favor," she said.

"Oh, I want advice, too," I said quickly. "I was wondering if you thought something like that would help? You know, get him to finally tell who his girl matchup is?"

Christie didn't say anything. That was a good sign, I thought. It probably meant that she was weakening. It did, and we talked for a long time. Before we hung up, she promised to talk me up to Randy, and we also said that we would start eating lunch together again.

Melanie was easier. I promised to talk her up to Scott Daly if she would talk me up to Randy. Katie said she would do it, too, but I could tell she thought it was silly.

I felt better than I had in ages. My four best friends and I were best friends again, and my campaign was going to work. Randy Kirwan was going to find out that I was still alive. Maybe he was embarrassed about being teased. And maybe he didn't want to hurt a lot of girls' feelings. And maybe he was getting conceited from all the attention. But he was still the most wonderful boy in the whole sixth grade.

I finished my homework quickly and started to turn on the television when a terrible thought occurred to me. I had promised Pink that I would talk him up to Mom, but so far I hadn't done it.

I could have gone into Mom's room right after I hung up from talking to him. Or I could have casually mentioned him while Mom and I ate supper. Or I could have said something about him when Mom told me that she was going to bed. Maybe she would be dreaming of Pink right now if I had done it then. I had meant to talk up Pink, but I had other things on my mind and I put it off. What if my four best friends put off talking me up to Randy, too?

My mind was racing as I dialed Beth's number again. "Beth!" I cried when she said hello. "When are you going to talk me up to Randy? And what are you going to say?"

"Gee, Jana. I don't know. I haven't really thought about it."

"Okay. Here's what I want you to do," I said. "Wait by the bike rack in the morning before school. When

Randy gets there, go over to him and say that I've been getting lots of calls from other boys. Tell him that you never realized before what a popular person I am. Say I'm so popular that my phone is ringing off the wall. Okay? Will you say that?"

"I guess so," said Beth. "Have you really been getting lots of calls?"

"Of course not. But if Randy thinks I'm popular, he might decide that he'd better do something about the competition."

Beth didn't say anything for a minute. "Do you really think it will work?"

"It will if you convince him that I'm the most popular girl in the sixth grade."

Next I called Christie. "Your locker is close to Randy's so here is what I want you to do," I instructed. "Get there early and get your books. Then when you see Randy at his locker, walk over casually and just mention how Taffy Sinclair is up to her old tricks. Tell him that she is so jealous of me for being so popular that she's trying to turn all the other sixth-grade girls against me."

"What do you mean 'for being so popular'?" asked Christie. "Is something going on that I don't know about?"

"Of course not. But I've got to make Randy think that there is. Can't you see that?"

"I guess so."

Melanie was perfect for the next thing I had in mind. "Your job is to convince Randy that I really am a kind and sensitive person," I said. "Go up to him at morning recess and tell him that on the way home from school today I saw a puppy in the middle of traffic and rescued him from being hit by a car. Randy is crazy about dogs. I know he'll be impressed."

"Jana, I didn't know that you rescued a puppy this afternoon."

I frowned at the receiver. "I didn't. But I'm always on the lookout for animals who need help. I would do it if I saw one. It's just that there isn't time to wait around for the real thing."

Melanie said she understood and that she would help me and we hung up. That left only Katie. She would be the hardest. I sat back and stared at the ceiling. Beth would make him jealous of the other boys and maybe he would even worry that I didn't like him anymore. Christie would make him see Taffy Sinclair for what she really is and feel angry about the way she is trying to turn everyone against me. Melanie would show him that I'm kind and care about animals, but what was left for Katie?

I racked my brain trying to think of something for Katie to say to Randy. Finally I decided to sleep on it, and I promised myself that I would talk up Pink to Mom first thing in the morning.

11 *

"**P**ink certainly is a thoughtful person, isn't he?" I said when Mom and I met at the breakfast table the next morning. "I think you should take your flowers to work with you today and set them on your desk so that he can see how much you appreciate them."

Mom looked at me and raised an eyebrow the way she always does when she says something like "You're nuts," or "I think you've flipped," except this time she didn't say anything because her mouth was full of toast.

"I mean, how many guys would be so concerned about your health? Not very many. He's someone you can really count on."

Mom took a drink of coffee and looked at me over the rim of her cup. "Why all this sudden interest in Pink?" she asked suspiciously.

"Oh, it isn't sudden," I assured her. "I've liked Pink ever since you started going out with him." Then I crossed my fingers behind my back for good luck and kept on talking. "Actually, I've always been very impressed with what a super person he is. And to think that now he even wants to take you to Ricardo's. You can tell that he really cares about you."

"Jana!" Mom exploded. "I'm tired of hearing about Pink. I'm also tired of taking his phone calls and accepting his flowers and hearing his marriage proposals. You might say that I'm just plain tired of Pink. Now may we please change the subject?"

"Sure. I have to leave for school anyway." At least I tried, I thought. I gave her a quick peck on the cheek as I grabbed my lunch off the counter and headed for the door.

Mom isn't cooperating one bit, I thought. Poor Pink. He was such a terrific guy and he really cared for her. How could she be so heartless? It would be different when my friends talked me up to Randy. He would be so impressed that he would see me for what I really am, and he would remember what a super time we had on our date.

As I walked along, I tried to picture Taffy Sinclair's face when Randy finally got around to announcing that he had my name all along. He would probably be on the playground, or maybe in the Media Center. Then he would look at me and smile that kind and sensitive smile and say, "I matched up with Jana Morgan because she is such a super person and we have so much in common. We were meant for each other." Then Taffy would start sobbing loudly, and I, being as kind and sensitive as Randy Kirwan, would say, "Poor Taffy Sinclair. We should all feel sorry for her."

My fabulous daydream was interrupted by the sudden thought that I still did not have anything specific for Katie to say to Randy. I hurried toward school. Maybe she would have some ideas.

When I got to school, the first person I saw was Beth, and she was hanging around the bike rack the way she was supposed to do. I had been watching her only for a minute when Randy came riding onto the playground. He was going so fast that I was sure he was going to run into the bike rack, but he hit his brakes, throwing gravel all over the place and stopping only about an inch from the rack.

I ducked behind a tree and watched Beth walk casually over to him. I was too far away to hear what they were saying and I wasn't very good at reading lips, so I just stood there watching and holding my breath.

"Jana Morgan. Why are you hiding behind that tree?"

It was Katie, and she startled me so badly that I jumped a foot off the ground.

"You didn't have to announce it to the whole world," I said, giving her a poison-dart look.

Katie looked past me to where Beth and Randy stood talking. "Oh, brother," she said. "Now I get it. Beth is over there giving Mr. Conceited the big word on how wonderful you are."

"So?" I said. "And don't call him Mr. Conceited. He happens to be a fantastic person."

Katie looked as if she was getting ready to say something else, but at that same moment Beth came running up. She was out of breath and grinning like crazy.

"I did it. I said everything you told me to say."

I collapsed against the tree with relief. "Great!" I said. "What did he say? Tell me everything."

Beth got a funny look on her face. "Well . . . he didn't actually say anything. He just sort of shrugged."

"That's probably because he didn't want you to see how jealous he is," I said. "Just wait. You'll see."

I avoided looking at Katie. I knew what she was probably thinking. It didn't matter. Nothing did, except getting Randy back.

Christie was waiting for him by the lockers just the way I had told her to do. I was so excited that my hands were shaking when I opened my own locker and got out my books. Once Christie got through with him, Randy would never speak to Taffy Sinclair again. And then at recess Melanie would convince him that I was kind to animals, especially small, helpless ones that were stuck in traffic. He would be so impressed that it wouldn't matter even if I couldn't think of a speech for Katie.

I didn't get a chance to talk to Christie before the bell rang so I slipped her a note during class. It said:

DEAR CHRISTIE:

WHAT DID YOU SAY TO RANDY AND WHAT DID HE SAY BACK?

LOVE,
JANA

A few minutes later she passed a note back to me. It said:

DEAR JANA:

I SAID WHAT YOU TOLD ME TO SAY ABOUT TAFFY SINCLAIR AND HE DIDN'T SAY ANYTHING. HE JUST SHRUGGED.

LOVE,
CHRISTIE

I read that note over and over, thinking about how Randy must be feeling. He had to realize that Taffy was a terrible person and that he had better ask me to go for pizza Saturday if he didn't want some other boy to ask me. I sighed. I almost wished that Melanie wasn't going to talk to him at morning recess. That would be a perfect time for him to come up and start talking to me. Of course there was still lunchtime, and we would have more time then.

At recess, I tried not to stare at Randy and Melanie, but I could see that they were deep in conversation. Melanie was doing all the talking and Randy was listening with a serious look on his face. It was working. I could tell, and when Randy and I were back together, I would have my best friends to thank.

I told my friends to go ahead to the cafeteria and get a table at lunchtime, and I stopped in the girls' bathroom to comb my hair and make sure I looked okay. I sighed, wishing I had sneaked some of Mom's lip gloss into my knapsack before I left home this morning. Then I combed my hair a second time and hurried toward the lunchroom. I knew that Randy was probably wondering where I was. My hands were so sweaty that the top of my lunchbag was getting damp as I went inside.

My friends were at our usual table, and I headed toward them trying to act casual and look for Randy at the same time. At first I didn't see him. All I saw was my friends. All four of them were frowning, and Beth was nodding toward the back of the room. I looked in that direction to see what they were all so upset about. I stopped cold. There was Randy Kirwan, and he was the only boy at a table full of girls.

My knees buckled, and I sat down beside Katie with a thud. I didn't look at my friends. I knew they would all be feeling sorry for me and have sympathetic looks on their faces. All I could see was Randy and that table full of girls. Lisa Snow. Alexis Duvall. Sara Sawyer. Kim Baxter. Mona Vaughn. And, of course, Taffy Sinclair. Randy was grinning like crazy and talking to those girls as if he were the biggest deal in the world. Taffy was sitting across from him and she was hanging on every word.

Suddenly I realized that I didn't really know Randy as well as I thought I did. In fact, I had been wrong about him all along. All of a sudden, I wanted to tell him so. I stood up and marched over to the table where he sat with all those girls.

Randy glanced up. Boy, did he look surprised when he saw me standing there. All the girls looked at me, too. Especially Taffy. She was glaring at me with poison-dart eyes. No one said anything. It was as if I were in the middle of a stage and the audience was waiting for me to begin my solo. I didn't care. I had something to say and I was going to say it.

"You think you are so wonderful, Randy Kirwan," I began. "Well, you aren't wonderful at all. You're conceited! In fact, you aren't just the most conceited boy in Mark Twain Elementary. You're the most conceited boy in the world!"

Randy's face flushed a bright red and he looked at me with a funny expression.

"And furthermore, you think it's such a big deal to keep your girl matchup a secret. You think girls will fall all over you to find out who it is. Well, maybe some of them will, but I won't! I don't care! In fact, I hope you didn't get me. I hope you got . . ." I fumbled for an instant trying to think of the worst possible person for him to match up with. ". . . WIGGINS!" I shouted triumphantly.

I felt so much better I thought I'd die, and I turned around and stomped back to my table. I knew that the cafeteria had gotten deathly quiet. I also knew that everybody was looking at me. I didn't care. I sat there laughing in my mind, thinking about Randy matching up with Wiggins and taking her to Mama Mia's for pizza Saturday after the football game.

"Pssst. Jana. Look!"

Randy was leaving the cafeteria, and he was walking out with Taffy Sinclair.

Every time I looked at Randy all afternoon, he was looking at Taffy Sinclair, and most of the time she was looking back. Well, she can have him, I thought. I don't know what I ever saw in him. I don't know why the computer gave me his name in the first place. That stupid computer made a big mistake. Romance Machine? Huh!

12 ✳

I could hardly wait for Mom to get home, and I met her at the door. "Boy, you should have heard me tell off Randy Kirwan in the cafeteria today," I bragged. "He thinks he's so smart. I don't know what I ever saw in him in the first place."

"Oh, hi, Jana," Mom said in a faraway voice. "How was your day?" She hung up her coat and glanced around, but she didn't really look at me. Instead, it was almost as if I were invisible and she was looking straight through me.

"I said, I really told off Randy Kirwan in the cafeteria," I repeated. It didn't register. She still had that blank stare so I went on, "and then I took Wiggins hostage and bombed the school."

"That's nice, dear," she said. "I'll call you when dinner's ready."

I was starting to get worried. This wasn't like her. "Earth to Mom. Earth to Mom. Come in. This is Jana."

Instantly her glazed look disappeared. "Oh, Jana. I'm so sorry," she said, and I could tell that she really meant it. "I've had a terrible day. Pink hasn't stopped by my desk to talk to me once today. He must be angry with me over something, but I can't imagine what. I'm worried sick. Now, what were you saying?" Her eyes suddenly opened wide. "There was a bomb threat at school!"

"No, Mom. I was only teasing. Didn't you have lunch with Pink? You two have lunch together almost every day."

Mom shook her head. "I saw him leaving the building at noon alone. I can't imagine what's wrong. I just hope he wasn't meeting another woman."

I could see that Mom was really upset, but for the life of me I couldn't understand her. "Mom?" I asked. "Aren't you the same person who was saying just this morning at breakfast that Pink was bugging the daylights out of you and that you didn't want to talk about him anymore?"

Mom looked sheepish. "I know that's what I said," she admitted. Then her eyes got misty. "But that was before he started ignoring me. I guess I didn't realize just how much he meant to me until now. I know this is going to sound strange, but I really miss him. If only he hadn't come on so strong before, practically suffocating me with attention. Maybe I would have seen him for what he really is. Kind . . . sensitive . . . caring."

She moved into the kitchen, still mumbling to herself about Pink. I shook my head and went to my room. Men! I thought. They either drove you nuts telling you how much they cared about you, like Pink used to do and like Curtis Trowbridge. Or else they ignored you altogether like Pink and Randy Kirwan were doing now. Women ought to get even with them, I thought. We ought to band together and go on strike!

When I walked to school the next morning I tried not to think about Randy and how it was Thursday, our one-week anniversary. Last Thursday was the day that he had called to ask me out for pizza after his football game. It seemed longer than a week ago. It seemed more like a year.

There's no use thinking about Randy anymore, I told myself. I took care of him yesterday.

I spotted my four best friends beside the swings. They were with a group of other girls, and they were all talking excitedly. I stopped when I saw who the other girls were. Lisa Snow, Sara Sawyer, Kim Baxter, and Alexis Duvall. All the girls who had been sitting with Randy in the cafeteria yesterday except for Mona Vaughn and Taffy Sinclair. What did they want? I wasn't sure I even wanted to find out.

Alexis saw me first, and she started smiling and waving like crazy for me to join the group. "Come here,

Jana," she called. "We have something important to tell you."

I hesitated for a moment, but then all the others started smiling and waving, including my four best friends, so I went over to see what was going on.

Everybody started talking at once. "You were right about Randy Kirwan," said Kim.

"He is the most conceited boy in Mark Twain Elementary," said Sara. "We should have seen it ourselves."

"But he's not the only boy who's conceited," Lisa added. "All the sixth-grade boys are."

I couldn't believe what I was hearing. "But all of you were sitting with Randy yesterday," I said. "You were acting as if you thought he was great."

"We did—*then*," said Alexis. "But we got to thinking about what you said to him, and we decided that all sixth-grade boys are jerks."

"Including Randy Kirwan," said Lisa. "And we don't care if any of them tell us who they matched up with. Where do they get off thinking they can just refuse to tell who their girl matchups are? Every one of them has some kind of ego problem, if you ask me."

"If they don't need us, we don't need them!" said Sara. "We ought to find some way to get even."

"Then you're not mad at me anymore?" I asked cautiously.

"Mad at you?" echoed Kim. "You're the one who opened our eyes."

"Not only that," added Melanie. "It took a lot of nerve to tell him off the way you did."

As I stood there listening, I suddenly remembered what I had been thinking yesterday after Mom told me about her troubles with Pink, and I got this great idea. "Why don't we go on strike?" I said.

"Strike?" asked Christie.

"Yeah," said Beth. "What do you mean?"

I smiled triumphantly. "Boys are always asking us for things. You know. Like borrowing things."

"Oh, I get it," said Melanie. "Things like notebook paper. Scott Daly never has notebook paper, and he's always borrowing it from me."

"And what about pencils?" asked Sara. "Either they don't have them at all or the points are broken off and they're too short to sharpen."

"Don't forget homework," added Katie.

"Especially math homework," said Kim.

Beth's face lit up and she said, "Just think. If we go on strike like Jana said, they'll have to bring their own stuff to school or they'll get in trouble, and they'll have to do their own homework."

"We'll teach them a thing or two," said Alexis. "And believe me, they really deserve it. Boys are such jerks."

"BOYS—ARE—JERKS! GIRLS—ON—STRIKE! BOYS—ARE—JERKS! GIRLS—ON—STRIKE!" someone started chanting. The rest of us tried to join in, but we were laughing so hard that we could barely stand up, and we almost didn't hear the bell.

By the time we went to our lockers and got our books, practically every girl in the sixth grade was in on our plan. You would have thought that Wiggins was in on the whole thing, too, because right after she took roll she cleared her throat and said, "All right, boys and girls. Get a clean sheet of paper and a pencil. We're going to have a spelling quiz on the words on page 56 of your spelling book."

I smiled to myself and got ready for what was about to happen. An instant later someone poked me on the left shoulder.

"Jana," whispered Clarence Marshall. "May I borrow a sheet of paper?"

I turned around slowly, gave him a huge sigh of boredom, and said, "Sorry, Clarence. I'm all out." Then I picked up my notebook and held it where he could see it and flipped through about a hundred sheets of blank paper.

Across the room Mark Peters got a panicked look on his face as both Alexis Duvall and Kim Baxter refused to lend him a pencil. Joel Murphy was poking through the wadded up sheets of paper in the wastebasket. Keith Masterson was attacking the pencil sharpener where the stub of a pencil he had pushed into it had disappeared. Even Mr. Conceited himself, Randy Kirwan, was rummaging through his desk looking for a sheet of paper that did not have writing or drawings of airplanes on both sides.

Naturally all the commotion didn't go unnoticed by Wiggins. "Class! What seems to be the problem? Have I asked the impossible?"

A few girls giggled, and most of the boys looked around helplessly. Finally Mark Peters spoke up.

"We need to borrow some paper and pencils, but none of the girls will lend us any," he said.

Wiggins didn't say anything for a minute, and I thought I could detect that she was struggling not to smile. Good old Wiggins, I thought. She understands.

She did understand. "Well, Mark," she said solemnly. "Why don't you boys have paper and pencils of your own? You know that it is your RESPONSI-BILITY to have them."

"I just ran out of paper yesterday," he offered.

"I left mine at home," said Joel.

"Me, too."

"Me, too."

"I broke my pencil when I fell off my bike."

Suddenly the air was full of boys shouting out excuses for not having any paper or pencils. Wiggins crossed her arms over her chest and listened to all of them. It was easy to see that she was unimpressed.

"Will all the boys who have no paper or pencil or both please raise your hands."

Slowly nine hands raised into the air.

Wiggins cocked an eyebrow. "All right. All nine of you may do your quizzes at the blackboard."

I was having a terrible time keeping a straight face. It was too good to be true. The boys were getting what they deserved.

Suddenly Taffy Sinclair's hand shot into the air. "Excuse me, Miss Wiggins," she said in her icky sweet voice. "I have lots of paper and pencils that the boys can borrow." Without waiting for Wiggins to answer, she gave Randy a piece of paper and a pencil and then handed a whole stack of paper and some more pencils to Mark Peters to pass around.

"Thanks a lot, Taffy. You're a real friend," said Mark.

"Yeah, thanks, Taffy," said Randy, and most of the other boys mumbled *thank-you*'s, too.

Taffy glanced over her shoulder at the rest of us. She had that nasty smile on her face that she always gets when she is feeling superior. We were all so mad that if poison-dart looks could kill, she'd have been a goner.

Wiggins tapped her foot impatiently as she waited for everyone to settle down. You could tell that she was disappointed, too. But leave it to Taffy Sinclair to mess things up. Anyway, when all the boys had their paper and pencils, she began calling out the spelling words.

"The last word is *responsibility*," Wiggins said loudly, sounding out all the syllables.

Responsibility? I thought. That wasn't on the list. Then I smiled to myself. Good old Wiggins.

After a couple of minutes we passed our spelling tests to the front, and Wiggins told us to get out our math books and begin working the problems on page 79. They were pretty easy. Multiplying decimals.

"Psst. Jana."

It was Keith Masterson. He always bugged me to give him answers, and sometimes I did. I smiled to myself. There was no way I was going to do it this time, and Taffy Sinclair was sitting too far away to help him.

"Jana," he whispered louder.

I kept right on ignoring him, and I could see all around the room that other girls were ignoring boys who wanted help with answers. Maybe our strike was going to work after all.

I should have known better than to forget about Taffy Sinclair. The moment Wiggins turned her back someone pitched a note onto Taffy's desk. I didn't see who did it, but it must have been a boy because Taffy was looking around and smiling her nasty smile again. Very slowly she started running the fingers of her left hand through the back of her long curly hair, acting as if she were concentrating on her problems. Then, when it was obvious that Wiggins wasn't looking, she held out three fingers, then two fingers, then made a fist, then one finger, and then she made a circle with her thumb and first finger.

It only took an instant to figure out what she was doing. I looked down the answers on my paper. Number seven! The answer I had gotten for number seven was 32.10. Taffy was giving the boys answers to the math problems. She had made the numbers three and two with her fingers. Her fist must have been the decimal point. Next she held up one finger and then made a circle for the zero. That traitor, I thought. I hated her more than ever.

On the playground after lunch Taffy Sinclair was the center of attention. The boys were all milling around her, talking and showing off. Every once in a while one of them would look away from Taffy and frown or throw a dirty look at any girl who went by. It was totally disgusting. Taffy Sinclair was batting her big blue eyes at them. I tried not to notice that the one she was batting her eyes at the most was Randy Kirwan.

My friends and I were standing with Alexis, Lisa, Sara, and Kim.

"They think that they are such hot stuff!" said Alexis. "Just wait. They can't get along without us forever."

I wasn't so sure. The way Taffy Sinclair had taken over made me wonder if any of them would ever notice us again.

Things really got out of hand when we got back to the room after lunch. As we were heading for our seats, Kim Baxter accidentally brushed her hand against Clarence Marshall's arm.

"Yuk!" shrieked Kim. "I touched a boy! Yuk! Yuk!"

Kim shrank away from Clarence and held out her hand as if it had poison on it. That was all it took.

"Yuk!" girls all over the room began to shout. "Yuk! Don't touch boys!"

With a big grin, Clarence lunged for Kim and slapped at her back, pretending to wipe something on her. Some of the other boys started doing the same thing, chasing girls around the room and trying to touch them while the girls were screaming "Yuk! Yuk!" at the top of their lungs.

Keith Masterson took out after me. He was making monster noises, and he grabbed my arm, nearly pulling it out of the socket.

"YUK!" I screamed and tried to wrench out of his grip.

Just then Wiggins walked into the room. We all froze as if we were playing statues and waited to see what she would do.

Wiggins drew herself up to her full height and strode to the center of the room. Sunlight streaming in the windows glinted off her glasses, making her eyes look like circles of fire. "Get into your seats immediately," she commanded, and we did.

"Will someone please explain to me what this little episode was all about?"

Of course nobody did. Nobody wanted to rat on their classmates. Not even Taffy Sinclair. Inside my chest my heart was pounding as if it were trying to get out.

"I'm waiting," Wiggins warned.

Still nobody said anything.

"If no one volunteers, I will pick one of you," she said. Then she began tapping her foot.

The room was so quiet that I could hear the electric clock humming. I had never heard that clock hum before. I tried to imagine what kind of punishment

Wiggins would come up with if nobody would tell. Just then I heard a voice.

"I'll explain what happened." It was nerd of the world, Curtis Trowbridge. Leave it to him to fink, I thought. He was beaming as if he was about to do the most noble thing in the world. "The girls started it."

Clarence Marshall scrambled to his feet. "That's right, Miss Wiggins. I just walked into the room minding my own business when Kim Baxter ran up to me and punched me and then started shouting 'Yuk! I touched a boy! Yuk!'"

"That's a lie!" shrieked Kim. "I didn't punch him. I just accidentally brushed against him. And then he punched ME in the back—really HARD—and it HURT." Kim started fake crying, and she doubled over as if she were in pain.

"The girls think they're so smart," said Mark Peters. "They walk around with their noses in the air and act like it's a really big crime if one of us wants to borrow a sheet of paper or something."

"They're the ones who think they're smart," shouted Alexis. "They don't even bother to bring their own paper and pencils to school or even do their homework. They expect us to take care of them. They're just a bunch of conceited babies!"

"I think I know what the matter really is," offered Randy. Then he looked straight at Wiggins and said, "They're mad because none of us will tell them who our girl matchup is. You said we didn't have to. You said we could keep it a secret if we wanted to."

"Sooooo," said Wiggins, glancing around the room with a sly expression. "Just as I expected. This entire episode has something to do with the computer matchup." She paused a moment. There was a gleam in her eye. "Yes, Randy. I did tell you that you could keep your matchups a secret if you wanted to. But there is something else about the computer that I did not mention."

Wiggins paused again, and I began to squirm in my seat. What on earth could she be talking about? Could the computer tell if you were lying? Or if you put down an answer because you thought it would make you match up with someone special? Or worst of all, since the boys were being so mysterious, did that mean the computer knew our secrets, and did it tell all our secrets to the boys?

13 ❊

What Wiggins said next was just about the strangest thing I had ever heard.

"In some ways, the computer is only human."

I wasn't the only one who thought it was strange. All over the room kids were shuffling their feet and shrugging and making weird faces at each other. Wiggins let us do that for a moment before she went on.

"Some of you have been acting like big shots, enjoying all the attention you got from keeping your matchups a secret and playing hard to get. Some of the rest of you have been making nuisances of yourselves by trying every trick you can think of to find out who those matchups are."

How did Wiggins know a thing like that? I wondered. Had she been spying? Did she know about how I had my friends talk me up to Randy Kirwan? Did she think I had made a nuisance of myself? I felt my ears start to get hot.

"Some of you have even been acting as if the computer were some sort of magic box that could tell you who your true love was meant to be. The truth, as I said, is that the computer is only human because it can only evaluate the information you give it. It doesn't know anything you don't tell it. So," she paused, sticking up a finger like an exclamation point, "the matchup each one of you got is exactly who you wanted."

I shot up straight in my seat and frowned at Wiggins. How could she say a thing like that? Randy Kirwan is the most conceited boy in the world. I certainly don't want anything to do with him, I thought. Then another voice in my mind spoke up. "You did when you filled out that questionnaire. Besides, what if he was just enjoying the attention he was getting from all the girls who got his name?" "Isn't that what *conceited* means?" reasoned the first voice. "Well, maybe he was just playing hard to get," said the second voice.

No! I insisted, almost saying the word out loud. Randy wasn't *playing* anything. He had changed. Maybe he wasn't conceited before, but he certainly was now.

My four best friends felt the same way I did about what Wiggins had said about the computer matchup.

"Wiggins must be crazy to think we'd believe that we all got who we wanted on the boy–girl matchup," said Christie on the way home from school. "If I had gotten who I wanted, I would have gotten Mr. Scott instead of Gregory Harper."

"I'd rather have Gregory Harper than who I got," I said. "Anybody is better than Randy Kirwan."

"I think she was just saying that to calm everybody down," said Katie. I tried not to laugh, remembering that Katie had gotten "Computer error #14."

I was still fuming about it when Mom got home from work. This time she stormed into the apartment, slamming the door so hard that the dishes rattled.

"You'll be happy to know that I broke my date with Pink for dinner at Ricardo's Saturday night," she said.

I couldn't for the life of me think why I would be happy with news like that, but when I said so, it set Mom off ranting and raving about Pink.

"I've really had it with that man," she said. "I don't know why I've wasted so much of my life on him. And to think, I was actually considering marrying him."

"What did he do this time?" I asked.

"He ignored me again today. That's what. You'd think that I was poison or something. I don't know why he's suddenly changed, but I've had it!"

"But how can you forget what a super guy Pink is?" I asked. "Don't you remember how concerned he was when you were sick? He sent you flowers and called all the time to see if you needed anything."

"Oh, I remember, all right," she said, nodding her head and frowning as if I had just reminded her of something terrible. "First he made a nuisance of himself by trying every trick he could think of to get my attention. And *now*—now he's playing hard to get!"

I didn't answer right away. Mom's words had hit me like a bucket of cold water. They were almost the same words Wiggins had used when she was talking about the way our class was acting ever since the computer matchup. *Nuisance. Trying every trick he could think of. Playing hard to get.* I didn't know when I had been more confused. I was certain that Pink hadn't changed. He was just desperate. I couldn't blame him for trying all those things on Mom. She certainly could be stubborn sometimes. I wanted to believe that Randy hadn't changed either, but I couldn't. There was just too much evidence convincing me that he had.

"If you think Pink is bad, you should see Randy Kirwan," I said. "Ever since I told him off, he's been hanging around Taffy Sinclair. If you ask me, they deserve each other."

"Believe me, men are all alike," Mom said in that warning tone she gets sometimes. "To make matters worse, I got a call from your father today."

My heart fluttered. "You did?" I whispered. "What did he want?" I tried not to hope that he had wanted to talk to me, and of course he hadn't.

"He called to tell me that he lost his job. It's his drinking again. Not only that, he asked me for money. He knows that we can barely get along as it is."

"What are you going to do?"

"I have a little saved. I guess I'll have to send it to him. He hinted that without money he'd lose his apartment, and knowing him, that's the same as saying that he'd come here and try to live off us. That's all I need on top of my troubles with Pink. Men!" mumbled Mom.

"Men!" I echoed, but I was tingling all over. I knew Mom was right. My father is an alcoholic, and it would be wrong for him to try to live off us. But something inside me was secretly wishing that he would come, just for a little while, so that we could get better acquainted. Besides, Mom said that men were all alike. If that was true, maybe I could tell him about how Randy has been acting, and he would understand and know what I should do.

On the way to school the next morning I was still thinking about my father's call and about what a jerk Randy had become when I heard someone running up behind me.

"Jana," called Melanie. "Wait up."

She was out of breath when she caught up with me, but that didn't stop her from talking excitedly between gulps of air. "Scott called me last night . . . and . . . oh, Jana, he told me that he got my name. He said he was tired of keeping his matchup a secret." She paused to take a deep breath. "And guess what? You did start something when you had a date with Randy! Scott asked me to meet him at Mama Mia's after the game."

I smiled weakly and tried to think of something to say, but I had a queasy feeling in the pit of my stomach.

"And guess what else?" Melanie burst out. "I almost forgot. Oh, wow! You'd kill me if I forgot this." Then she lowered her voice to a confidential tone. "I asked Scott about Randy. Scott said that at first Randy didn't tell because he just didn't like all the attention. You know, the boys teasing him and all the girls saying they had his name and everything. He thought that he'd wait a while until things quieted down to tell who he got. But instead of quieting down, things got worse."

"You mean, he got conceited," I grumbled. "Did you ask him whose name Randy got?"

Melanie nodded. "He wouldn't tell me. He said that Randy would tell himself when he got ready."

We walked the rest of the way to school in silence. I didn't want to talk about Randy anymore. I felt so confused and hurt and angry that I didn't want to talk about anybody or anything.

All day long I kept hearing about boys who were telling girls that they got their name. Of course Clarence Marshall was going around saying he had Taffy. I also kept noticing that Randy was looking at me a lot, and once in the cafeteria he even tried to get my attention. I just looked the other way. I certainly didn't want to talk to him.

At home that evening I bragged to Mom about how I had snubbed Randy. "I wouldn't look at him once all day long," I said. "Not even when he tried to get my attention. I guess I showed him a thing or two."

"Don't you think you're being a little hard on him?" she asked. "It wasn't so long ago that you thought he was just about perfect, and I've always liked him. Maybe if you gave in and talked to him, all this trouble would be over with. Did you ever stop to think that maybe he's waiting for you to make the first move?"

I couldn't believe what I was hearing. How could she say a thing like that? After all, she had been having as much trouble with Pink as I had been having with Randy.

I looked at her suspiciously. "Did you pay attention to Pink today?"

Mom seemed embarrassed. "Not much," she said.

"What do you mean, not much?"

"Um . . . well, I said hello a couple of times, but that's all."

I was feeling confused again. Why did she keep changing her mind? I was certain that Pink really was a super person and that Mom had been mean to him the last couple of days. But now that she seemed to be giving in and talking to him again, I suddenly felt alone and betrayed. Just then the phone rang. It's probably Pink, I thought, feeling lonelier than ever. It wasn't. It was Melanie, and she wanted me to go to the boys' football game with her Saturday.

"I wouldn't go to that football game if it were the last thing left on earth to do," I said stubbornly.

"Oh, come on, Jana. It's going to be the best time ever. I caught Scott looking at me four times today, and Mark

Peters told Alexis that he got her name. He talked to her after school."

"Big deal," I grumbled. "Curtis Trowbridge already told me that he got my name, too. So what?"

"You're impossible," said Melanie. "Can't you see that all the boys are getting tired of keeping their matchups a secret? I'll bet Randy is getting tired of it, too."

I didn't answer. Then I heard Melanie sigh.

"You'd better change your mind and go to the game," she said. "Everybody will be there. Especially Taffy Sinclair."

After we hung up I thought over what Melanie had said. She was right about one thing. Everybody would be at the game. And even though I didn't want Randy anymore, it would be the same as handing him over to Taffy on a silver platter if I didn't show up. I couldn't do a thing like that. I would go to the game, but I would ignore Randy Kirwan. I would ignore him if it killed me.

14 *

I nearly jumped out of my skin when the phone rang again after dinner. I didn't want to talk to anyone so I pretended not to hear it. After it rang a couple of times, Mom answered.

"Hello," she said in her regular voice. A minute later I noticed that she was practically whispering, and when I looked at her she gave me a sheepish grin and disappeared into the closet with the phone the way I always do when I want some privacy. I shook my head. She was acting just like a teenager instead of a mother. Did love have that effect on grown-ups, too?

I didn't know when I'd ever been so nervous. It had to be Pink on the phone. What were they talking about that was so private? I didn't think they were fighting. At least I couldn't hear Mom yelling through the closet door.

What seemed like ages later Mom came out. There was a glow on her face and her eyes were shining. She sat down cross-legged on the sofa and just looked at me as a smile spread across her face. "I decided to forgive him," she said with an embarrassed shrug. "You'll probably think I'm crazy, but I said I'd go to Ricardo's with him tomorrow night."

I just stared at her. She had been so angry at him. How could she change her mind so quickly?

"What do you mean, you decided to forgive him?" I asked.

"Talking to him made me realize that I was only being stubborn because I was hurt, and I was hurt because he was playing hard to get. He admitted that he was being stubborn, too, and playing hard to get because I wasn't responding to all his attention. So because we were both so stubborn, we almost spoiled our chance to be happy together."

Mom's so lucky, I thought. If only Randy Kirwan were as super a person as Pink.

"There is one thing I didn't talk to him about, though," she said, and her eyes clouded. "Your father." Then her face brightened again and she reached out, giving my hand a warm squeeze. "But we'll worry about that when the time comes," she said in a cheerful voice. Still, I couldn't help feeling a little bit funny right now.

❋ ❋ ❋

The next morning was Saturday. When I called Melanie to tell her that I had decided to go to the game after all, she let out such a whoop that it almost blew out my left eardrum, cleared a path through my brain, and came out the other side of my head.

"But don't think I'm going to pay any attention to Randy Kirwan," I warned.

"Sure," she said in a tone that told me she didn't believe a word I said.

"I mean it. I've had it with that boy."

After we agreed to meet by the gate at the junior high football field, I started getting ready. I had washed my favorite jeans and my best top the night before. My sneakers were a cruddy mess, but maybe nobody would notice them. Just as I was tying my sneakers, Mom knocked on my bedroom door.

"I'm heading for the supermarket and the cleaners," she called. "Have fun at the game."

"Thanks," I called back.

As soon as I heard the front door close, I raced to the bathroom and plugged in Mom's curling iron. Then I dabbed on a tiny bit of her lip gloss. I wasn't really fixing up for anyone. It was just that my hair looked nicer curled and the gloss would keep my lips from getting chapped.

My four best friends were waiting by the gate when I got there. Melanie was dancing around, hopping from one foot to the other.

"Isn't this exciting?" she said. "I can hardly wait to go to Mama Mia's."

I couldn't help but think about last Saturday when I had been the one with the special date. If only the computer matchup had never happened. Then maybe Randy would not have become so conceited, and we would be going to Mama Mia's, too.

My friends and I headed for the section of the bleachers where all the kids sat. I kept my eyes down as we climbed up toward the top. I didn't want to talk to anyone.

"Hello, Jana." It was Taffy Sinclair, and she was using her icky sweet voice. "Are you going to Mama Mia's after the game?"

Taffy and Mona were sitting beside the stairway. They were both looking at me as if I were the Creature from the Black Lagoon. Taffy was wearing lavender slacks—lavender is her favorite color—and the most gorgeous white rabbit fur jacket I had ever seen. Sunlight shone in her blond curls, and I remembered self-consciously the botched-up job I had done with Mom's curling iron.

"What's it to you?" I snapped.

Taffy only shrugged and glanced toward the field, where our team had just appeared and were lining up for their warm-up. I stomped on up the stairs and sat down with my friends. Who did Taffy think she was, anyway? She was probably going to flirt her head off with Randy at Mama Mia's, and she wanted to make sure I would be there to see it.

I sneaked a look down at the field, where the team was doing jumping jacks, and my eyes just automatically zeroed in on Randy. The red number twenty-two seemed to stand out on his white uniform more than anyone else's on the team. At just that moment he looked up at me and flashed that 1,000-watt grin. I looked away quickly, even though I could feel my heart doing flip-flops the way it always did when he smiled at me. I could also hear a little voice in my mind. It was Mom, and she was confessing that she had been stubborn and that she was forgiving Pink.

Well, I'm not being stubborn, I told myself. It's Randy's fault. He's the one who has changed.

In a few minutes the referee signaled for the game to begin, and I sat there wishing I had never come. I tried not to watch what was going on on the field, but I couldn't help it. Every time our team had the ball, the quarterback threw it to Randy. And every time that happened, he ran toward the end zone and got jumped on by a zillion guys from the other team.

Finally, it was late in the fourth quarter. The score was tied, and our team had the ball down by the end zone. I was determined not to watch this time, so I stared as hard as I could at the back of Taffy Sinclair's head. I wished my eyes could bore right through her curly perm and into her brain and tell her what I thought of the way she acted.

Just then Katie poked me in the ribs. "Look, Jana. It's Randy. He's hurt."

My heart stopped. I could see someone in a white uniform lying on the ground. A bunch of other players were gathered around him, but they all scattered when the coach and his assistant ran onto the field. The two men bent over him, but he didn't move.

"Are you sure it's Randy?" I whispered, but already I had scanned the players standing along the sidelines and knew that number twenty-two was not among them.

"I saw him get tackled," said Katie. "It was awful. They hit him really hard."

It was as if time stood still as I watched the coach bending over Randy, but the scene became more and more blurry as tears filled my eyes. Randy was hurt. I couldn't believe this was really happening. Finally the coach and his assistant helped Randy to his feet and guided him toward the bench, walking on either side of him like a pair of human crutches. I closed my eyes and said a little prayer that he would be all right.

Suddenly I heard somebody scream. I opened my eyes and saw Taffy Sinclair jump to her feet. Her face was positively green, and she was pointing toward Randy.

"Blood!" she shrieked. "He's bleeding! Yuk! Blood!"

I gasped. Blood was pouring down his face and onto his jersey.

"It's just a bloody nose, everybody! Don't get excited," Curtis called up to the stands. Then he began scribbling furiously in his notebook, and I knew that Randy's bloody nose would make the front-page headline in the next *Mark Twain Sentinel*.

The coach helped Randy sit down on the bench and put his head between his knees. The water boy plopped an ice pack on the back of his neck, and the referee announced that our team had scored a touchdown on that play.

Taffy Sinclair streaked down the stairs and disappeared behind the bleachers.

"I'll bet she's going to throw up," Christie said gleefully. "She can't stand the sight of blood."

I smiled and tried to stand up and look in the direction Taffy had gone, but my legs had turned to jelly. "Randy's going to be okay," I mumbled to no one in particular.

Randy stayed on the bench for the rest of the game, even after his nose stopped bleeding. I allowed myself to look at him once or twice after I reminded myself that it was only natural to be concerned about anyone who got hurt.

I was probably the only one who noticed that Taffy Sinclair never came back to the game, and that Mona Vaughn had disappeared too. All the way to Mama Mia's all anyone could talk about was what a hero Randy had been for getting hurt and for scoring the winning touchdown at the same time.

My friends and I were practically the first ones to get from the game to Mama Mia's. We planned to get a table near the door, where we could watch everybody come in. As soon as we stepped inside we stopped cold. There was Taffy Sinclair. She and Mona Vaughn had already gotten the best table in the place, the one closest to the door.

"Hello, Jana," she said in her icky sweet voice. She was smiling that nasty smile of hers. "Don't you have a date with Randy today?"

I knew what she was getting at. She might as well have gone ahead and said that it proved that Randy didn't have my name after all. I didn't answer her. I couldn't. I might have said something awful if I had.

"Come on, Jana." Beth was pulling on my sleeve. "Just ignore her. We have to find a table before they're all gone."

I looked around, and Beth was right. Kids were streaming in all over the place. We finally found a table near the back of the room. The only thing good about it was that it was close to the big round table where the football team usually sat.

A couple of minutes later a cheer went up as the football team came in. I knew they had to walk right past Taffy Sinclair to get to their regular table. I couldn't stand to look.

"I'm going to sit with Scott now," chirped Melanie. "I'll see you later."

She jumped up and ran over to the table where the boys were sitting. I stole a glance at Randy. He was a little pale and his nose was red, but otherwise he looked as handsome as ever. Lots of kids were congratulating him and telling him how sorry they were about his nose. He just kept shrugging and saying that it was no big deal.

Suddenly my heart felt as if it would explode. I had been so worried when he was hurt, and now he was acting as if it were nothing at all. Maybe Randy wasn't quite as conceited as I had thought. Maybe I was being stubborn because I was hurt when he played hard to get and wouldn't tell who he got for his matchup. I thought about Mom and Pink. They had both been stubborn, but everything had turned out super when Mom decided to forgive him and not to be so stubborn herself anymore. Maybe Randy and I had both been a little bit stubborn too.

I sat there for a long time, shredding the paper napkin in my lap and thinking about Randy. I knew he was looking at me. When I finally looked back at him, not only was he smiling his 1,000-watt smile, but there was an empty chair beside him and a large deep-dish pepperoni, green pepper, and mushroom pizza on the table. I checked my tongue, but it wasn't the least bit numb, so I took a deep breath and slowly stood up.

"Where are you going?" asked Katie.

"To sit with Randy," I said, and when she got a puzzled look on her face, I added, "I've decided to forgive him."

❁   ❁   ❁

We had a super time at Mama Mia's. I was so happy to be with Randy again that I almost forgot to look at Taffy Sinclair, but of course I did. It was just a little look. More of a peek. But she was certainly looking at me, and from the awful expression on her face you would have thought she had just swallowed a swarm of wasps. The next time I peeked, she and Mona were gone.

On the way home Randy admitted that he had been mad at first when I called him "conceited" but that it had started him thinking. Of course there were several things that he didn't admit. Like how he had been playing hard to get and how much he liked the attention he got from all the other girls, but that was all right. If there was one thing I had learned, it was that he wasn't perfect. Well, not *totally* perfect anyway. Just wonderful.

"Do you know what else?" he asked as we stood on my front step to say good-bye.

"What?"

"Remember how Wiggins said that the name we got was the one we really wanted?"

I nodded.

Randy grinned. "I had your name all along." Then before I could answer, he leaned forward and kissed me on the lips.

I stood there for a long time after he left. I could still feel that kiss. I hugged myself and thought about how I had sneaked Randy's straw as a souvenir of our first date. I didn't need souvenirs anymore. I had the real thing. I had Randy Kirwan, the most wonderful boy in the world.

ABOUT THE AUTHOR

BETSY HAYNES, the daughter of a former news-woman, began scribbling poetry and short stories as soon as she learned to write. A serious writing career, however, had to wait until after her marriage and the arrival of her two children. But that early practice must have paid off, for within three months Mrs. Haynes had sold her first story. In addition to a number of magazine short stories and the Taffy Sinclair series, Mrs. Haynes is the author of *The Great Mom Swap* and *The Great Boyfriend Trap*. She lives in Colleyville, Texas, with her children and husband, a businessman who is the author of a young adult novel.

☐ **TAFFY SINCLAIR AND THE**   **15494/$2.50**
ROMANCE MACHINE DISASTER
by Betsy Haynes

Taffy Sinclair is furious. Her rival, Jana Morgan, has a date with Randy Kirwan, the most popular boy at school. When their teacher conducts a computer match-up game, Jana and 9 other girls, including Taffy turn out to be just right for Randy. Jana vows to win him! But is she any match for Taffy?

☐ **THE AGAINST TAFFY**   **15413/$2.50**
SINCLAIR CLUB
by Betsy Haynes

It was bad enough when Taffy Sinclair was just a pretty face. But now she's gone and developed a figure! This calls for drastic measures from the Against Taffy Sinclair Club made up of Jana Morgan and her four fifth-grade friends.

☐ **TAFFY SINCLAIR**   **15645/$2.75**
STRIKES AGAIN
by Betsy Haynes

It is time gorgeous Taffy Sinclair had a little competition. That's what Jana and her friends decide to give her when they form a club called The Fabulous Five. But when the club's third meeting ends in disaster, Jana finds she has four new enemies!

☐ **TAFFY SINCLAIR,**   **15647/$2.75**
QUEEN OF THE SOAPS
by Betsy Haynes

What could be worse? The snooty but perfectly gorgeous Taffy has done it again—she's won a part in a soap opera to play a beautiful girl on her deathbed. Nothing like this ever happens to Jana Morgan or her friends, and they're not going to stand being upstaged one more time!

Buy them at your local bookstore or use this handy coupon for ordering:

Bantam Books, Dept. SK6, 414 East Golf Road, Des Plaines, IL 60016

Please send me the books I have checked above. I am enclosing $_____ (please add $2.00 to cover postage and handling). Send check or money order—no cash or C.O.D.s please.

Mr/Ms _____

Address _____

City _____ State/Zip _____

SK6—7/88

Please allow four to six weeks for delivery. This offer expires 1/89.

IT ALL STARTED WITH THE

Francine Pascal introduces you to Jessica and Elizabeth when they were 12, facing the same problems with their folks and friends that you do.

☐ BEST FRIENDS #1	15421/$2.50
☐ TEACHER'S PET #2	15422/$2.50
☐ THE HAUNTED HOUSE #3	15446/$2.50
☐ CHOOSING SIDES #4	15459/$2.50
☐ SNEAKING OUT #5	15474/$2.50
☐ THE NEW GIRL #6	15475/$2.50
☐ THREE'S A CROWD #7	15500/$2.50
☐ FIRST PLACE #8	15510/$2.50
☐ AGAINST THE RULES #9	15518/$2.50
☐ ONE OF THE GANG #10	15531/$2.50
☐ BURIED TREASURE #11	15533/$2.50
☐ KEEPING SECRETS #12	15538/$2.50
☐ STRETCHING THE TRUTH #13	15554/$2.50
☐ TUG OF WAR #14	15550/$2.50
☐ THE OLDER BOY #15	15556/$2.50
☐ SECOND BEST #16	15563/$2.50
☐ BOYS AGAINST GIRLS #17	15571/$2.50
☐ CENTER OF ATTENTION #18	15581/$2.50
☐ THE BULLY #19	15595/$2.50

Bantam Books, Dept. SVT, 414 East Golf Road, Des Plaines, IL 60016

Please send me the books I have checked above. I am enclosing $_____ (please add $2.00 to cover postage and handling). Send check or money order—no cash or C.O.D.s please.

Mr/Ms _____

Address _____

City/State _____ Zip _____

SVT—10/88

Please allow four to six weeks for delivery. This offer expires 4/89.

☐ THE SARA SUMMER 15600/$2.75
by Mary Downing Hahn
Twelve-year-old Emily Sherwood has grown like a beanstalk and all the kids are calling her "Giraffe." What's worse, her best friend has deserted her. Things seem pretty bad until Sara, a tall, tough, wacky and wise New Yorker teaches Emily a thing or two about life.

☐ YOU'RE GOING OUT THERE A 15577/$2.50
KID, BUT YOU'RE COMING BACK A STAR
by Linda Hirsch
Margaret Dapple is ten years old and tired of waiting around to grow up, tired of waiting for everyone—especially her parents and big sister Barbara—to recognize that she is not a baby anymore. So Margaret decides to show them all—she's going to improve her image.

☐ NOW IS NOT TOO LATE 15548/$2.75
by Isabelle Holland
When Cathy arrives on the island to spend the summer with her grandmother, her summer friends warn her to stay away from the Wicked Witch, who turns out to be hauntingly familiar and not a witch at all.

☐ THE SISTERS IMPOSSIBLE 26013/$2.50
by J. D. Landis
As sisters go, Saundra and Lily have never been the best of friends. But the real trouble starts when their father buys younger sister Lily a pair of dancing shoes so she can go to ballet school with the beautiful and accomplished Saundra.

☐ ANASTASIA KRUPNIK 15534/$2.75
by Lois Lowry
To Anastasia Krupnik, being ten is very confusing. On top of everything her parents are going to have a baby—at their age! It's enough to make a kid want to do something terrible . . .

Buy them at your local bookstore or use this handy coupon for ordering:

Bantam Books, Dept. SK5, 414 East Golf Road, Des Plaines, IL 60016

Please send me the books I have checked above. I am enclosing $_____ (please add $2.00 to cover postage and handling). Send check or money order—no cash or C.O.D.s please.

Mr/Ms _____

Address _____

City/State _____ Zip _____

SK5—4/88

Please allow four to six weeks for delivery. This offer expires 10/88.

☐ **MISS KNOW IT ALL**   15408/$2.25

☐ **MISS KNOW IT ALL RETURNS**   15351/$2.25
by Carol Beach York
Miss Know It All appears suddenly one morning on the door-step of the Good Day Home for Girls. All 28 girls are amazed at all Miss Know It All knows. But something happens to make the girls fear that they will lose their wonderful Miss Know It All forever! Both these warm and delightful books are a must to read.

☐ **HELP, THERE'S A CAT**   15374/$2.50
WASHING IN HERE
by Alison Smith
Henry Walker has a choice: he can keep house for his youn-ger brother and sister while his mother is busy or else horrible Aunt Wilhelmina will come to stay. Henry decides to take charge, but he wasn't prepared for Kitty, a 20-pound yellow-eyed monster cat.

☐ **JACOB TWO-TWO MEETS**   42255/$2.75
THE HOODED FANG
by Mordechai Richler
Jacob Two-Two says everything twice because no one listens to him the first time. But then he is convicted of insulting a grown-up and exiled to Slimer's Isle—a nightmarish prison guarded by wolverines and slithering snakes and the dreaded Hooded Fang!

☐ **OWLS IN THE FAMILY**   15585/$2.50
by Farley Mowat

This is the hilarious true tale of two Saskatchewan owls; Wol is a wonderful bird that terrorizes everyone, and Weeps is a comical bird afraid of almost everything, except a dog named Mutt. There are laughs galore as these two shake up a neighborhood, turn a house topsy-turvy and even outsmart Mutt!

☐ **ARTHUR THE KID**   15169/$2.25
by Alan Coren

When the bumbling Black Hand Gang, the goofiest outlaws in the Wild West, advertise for a boss, who do they get? Arthur the Kid, of course!

Prices and availability subject to change without notice.
Buy them at your local bookstore or use this handy coupon for ordering:

Bantam Books, Dept. SK8, 414 East Golf Road, Des Plaines, IL 60016

Please send me the books I have checked above. I am enclosing $_____ (please add $2.00 to cover postage and handling). Send check or money order—no cash or C.O.D.s please.

Mr/Ms _____

Address _____

City _____ State/Zip _____

SK8—4/88

Please allow four to six weeks for delivery. This offer expires 10/88.